The Legend Begins

Book I

The Legend Begins

Book I

Peter W. Costigan

Dedication

To my Dad. Thank you for marrying my Mom, taking in six children and leaving me with a younger brother, an exact replica of you. Working Wednesday nights cleaning with you, hot cocoa on the US Coast Guard Cutter Duane, and most memorable, the example of fatherhood you instilled in me.

Miss you!

Foreword

It has been my delight to have known Peter for over fifty years, first as my kid brother and later as a remarkable mature man. I've also had the joy of watching Peter grow in his personal relationship with the Lord Jesus Christ. I have also been impressed with how, as a single father, Peter was always wholly dedicated to his three children, who have all grown to be such a joy and blessing to everyone.

In addition to Peter's passion for his family and the Lord, he has had an undying love for hockey, having played the sport as a goalie for a large Boston high school. Subsequently, he became a huge fan of his home team, the Boston Bruins, year by year watching games on television, purchasing season tickets, and occasionally traveling to other cities to support his team.

Ten years ago, however, Peter found himself pursuing a new passion, all a result of an unusual comment once made to him by a printer with whom he had been working on a project. He remarked that Peter really "thinks outside the box." This piqued Peter's curiosity and so he promptly researched the phrase. He was surprised by innumerable references to the *Jack in the Box* toy. Consequently, he became fixated on the toy figure named Jack. It kept gnawing at him even though he couldn't comprehend the reason for this preoccupation.

Hockey became a little less important to Peter as he now made the decision to dedicate all of his spare time digging for any information about the origins of the *Jack in the Box* toy. Despite all of his time and effort, he could not find any definitive story, only a couple of theories. Eventually, it became obvious to Peter that he needed to address this nagging obsession. In time, he assembled a support staff which enabled him to pursue his desire to write The Legend of Jack book series.

This story takes place in a medieval setting. Interestingly, however, it mirrors our lives today with issues such as war, pestilence, and government intrusion and control through fear, all resulting in a deep rift in society.

Of course, it is all about good versus evil. It displays human acts of heroism, self-sacrifice, love of freedom, and the forces hell-bent on destroying everything that is good. You will encounter episodes filled with suspense, intrigue, subtle humor, imagination and magic. You'll find colorful characters with whom you will identify. This writing is just plain good old-fashioned fun, and the ending will leave you wanting to read more.

Now, **you** don't know Jack. People sense that Jack is different; he has an endearing quality for greatness, if not heroic. There is a look in his eyes that gives the impression that somehow he is destined for greatness. Because of his apparent goodness, there are those who are always willing to provide Jack with aid and those who hate him and seek his destruction. Meanwhile, this troubled world that Jack was born into groans for The One to come and save them. Could that One be Jack?

Ironically, Peter himself is a "jack of all trades" having successfully studied and worked as an auto mechanic, chef, carpenter, and currently as a building contractor. Having had no actual experience with the art of writing, however, it is obvious that Peter has a natural talent for storytelling, clearly exhibited by Book One in the series, *"The Legend Begins."*

Preface

It is a familiar toy: the crank fixed to the box's side plays the jaunty and familiar tune when little hands turn it. It tinkles away, charmingly. After the first time, there is childish anticipation, knowing what will happen but ready to be startled, ready for the surprise that is not a surprise any longer, but still thrilling. And then — "Pop!!" The lid flies open as the figure — who? … a man? …a little boy? — with its clownish face and its thin flimsy body of a covered coiled spring emerges all at once. With much fanfare, its white-gloved hands flail at the end of its short arms and its head bobs wildly to and fro. Then comes the peals of laughter! The little child is delighted, even if it is the hundredth time. The adults are duly shown the trick. Even though the joke has been lost on them for a very long time, they keep laughing along with the little child.

The first time is very different. The little child is nonplussed at first. The music is delightful, the crank is charming, the little hand working it is participating. Here, the stares of the grown- ups huddled around are filled with anticipation, making the little child puzzled. What are they waiting for? What more is there than the crank and the music and the box itself, seemingly sealed up tight… a blank and impenetrable cube? We know, but the little child does not. When the box top springs open and the painted man spills out, the little child perhaps has his first taste of betrayal of good intentions gone awry.

The child's reaction might be a measure of the kind of adult the child may become, telegraphing latent traits. Most children are terribly startled and burst into tears straight away. Some are paralyzed for a moment, unable to decide one way or another what this new shock means. Some will attack, flailing tiny fists not yet completely controlled. And some, the brave ones, simply laugh along. Whatever the case, the box with the man inside teaches us the first and most valuable lessons of life: that is, things are not always as they appear. Danger can lurk in even the most seemingly innocuous places.

Does the memory stay with us? Perhaps it does, but the toy itself rarely does. Eventually we put away childish things and embark upon our own journeys, replete with trials and tribulations, as the playthings of the past fade from our memories and are left to themselves in rubbish heaps or in dusty attics. Yet curiously, they have a history of their own, a journey of their own, whether we are there to see it or not...

Have you ever really thought about the joker inside the box? No one seems to be able to recall his story. Questions upon questions begin to arise such as: Where does he come from? Where does he go? And most of all, why does he dwell there? Who has trapped him in this way and for what purpose? What will happen to him in the end? Will he attain great joy, or fall before a host of enemies?

If you are intrigued, then read on. What questions you have may be answered; but be warned! You may be left with only more questions. This is a story of the fantastic living behind the mundane. This is a story of a little boy: orphaned but not abandoned and thrust into a world of magic and mystery with only his cunning and courage to see him through. His story is one of a hero despite his humble beginnings. Who could have foreseen such a future for the boy trapped in the box? This is the story of Jack...

The Legend Begins...

 long time ago, deep in your imagination, lived twin sisters, Mara and Darcia. A stranger would never know that they were born out of the same womb for these two sisters were different in every way. The eldest, Mara, possessed and practiced the art of black magic, so fitting to her personality. She mastered the art and used it selfishly only to further her desire to rule over people and, even better, the entire world. Darcia, on the other hand, practiced white magic since she believed in *"harming none."* With her powers, she hoped to honor her father and the kingdom.

They were the daughters of King Wessex, the ruler of the kingdom of Hagen. At that time, this was the largest kingdom in the world, not only in size, but also by population. In fact, it was five times larger than the next biggest kingdom. Hagen's army was the largest and most advanced in the world. In the wrong hands, it was thought that it could easily wage war on the world and conquer it in less than a year. For one to have such power at their command, the choice would forever be whether to use this might for evil or for good.

King Wessex chose the latter, which proved difficult at times. No example of this was any more evident than having to pass this power on to his oldest daughter before he should die. There is a law in Hagen that rules succession, as with any other hereditary monarchy, wherein the firstborn would inherit the power. Thus, the family name could carry forward and the kingdom would survive. Like royal lineage, this power was passed on in this way to ensure that it was bound by blood, and not through marriage or any societal position. The course of Hagen, and the world for that matter, were about to be dramatically altered due to the order of the sisters' births. Mara was the first to see the light of day and, therefore, first in line for the throne, much to her father's chagrin. Darcia was, of course, born a close second, which proved meaningless as long as her sister was alive.

The sisters grew older; Darcia was the more beautiful of the two and Mara was the more cunning. It was said that twins were known to be cut from the same cloth. This exception, however, will make history and debunk that myth forever. As time went on, a rift between the two of them widened. Not only was it tearing them apart, but the kingdom as well. As they matured, Mara became more jealous of her sister. Darcia was a beautiful woman, almost perfect in every way. Mara was also pretty, but it wasn't in the same manner. Darcia's beauty transcended her outward looks. She could enter a room and a sense of calm would precede her, like that of a crisp spring morning or a light snow blanketing the landscape. People were drawn to her personality. This tore at Mara's insides. She became increasingly jealous as the years went by. It went markedly beyond which one was more beautiful than the other; no, the rift was much deeper than that. The seed of division was sown and watered in the womb. It was fate. This seed of malice took root within Mara's very soul, poisoning her whole body and spirit as well. Darcia kept her distance, always watching from afar, only to observe how her sister's actions would destroy people's lives and divide the Kingdom against itself. From time to time, she would come out of the shadows and secretly reverse the evil doings of Mara. Her sister always had her suspicions but could never prove it.

How could two sisters, born just minutes apart, be so different? Mara would incite and instigate arguments in public, in the royal residence, and in her favorite setting, the king's court, where all her father's assembly would witness it. This created a wedge between father and daughter. She was completely oblivious as to how much it pained him inwardly. Darcia would only be able to watch as his health and spirit diminished squarely due to Mara's continual assault on the family's name and the kingdom.

This was Mara's sadistic routine every day; that is, until the Great Plague struck. The plague brought out an evil never seen before, rising from within mankind's soul. At first Mara resented the fast-spreading disease but, in time she realized it mirrored her exact attitude towards the world. In a twisted way she greeted it as a guest. This undetectable killer, just too small to see with the naked eye, spread like a bad rumor in a social club. There were unforeseeable consequences that arose out of the plague. Hagen and the other kingdoms immediately plunged into fierce battle, driven by famine and lack of resources. The land was devastated. Water was poisoned. Pestilence was everywhere. The sisters' ongoing personal war was now overshadowed by the current great disease, blacked out by the cloud of death and despair that blanketed the world.

All the kingdoms waged war against one another, each for their own survival. This went on for a while with no one emerging as the victor. The death toll rose. Finally, between the kingdoms of Hagen and Windermere, the closest foes geographically, both being on opposite sides of Grim Rock, a tentative agreement was made, and an uneasy peace was brokered — much to Mara's dismay. She absolutely wanted her father to crush not only Windermere, but all the kingdoms that remained. Nevertheless, this agreement influenced the other kingdoms, causing each one to retreat within its own borders and thereby isolating themselves from the rest of the world. As a result, war ceased but the plague raged on.

To keep the peace, the kingdoms of Hagen in the east and Windermere in the west agreed to establish a neutral zone, using soldiers from each side to enforce it. The Great Council was formed. Three representatives from each kingdom were appointed to govern this area. A seventh, tie-breaking seat was voted on by the citizens from each kingdom. This seat was named "The Decider" by the people who lived in the Neutral Zone. The two Kingdoms were allowed to choose two people to represent them in the voting process for this coveted seat. This seemingly worked well for the first few years, but then it became evident that Mara bought off or blackmailed those who ran for and won this highly sought-after seat on the great Council. Typically, no one dared to confront her; but on the rare occasion when someone would, that person was straight-a-way never to be heard from or seen again.

This Neutral Zone quickly filled with shops and houses, developing into its own peculiar city. It became a place of intrigue, where cultures mixed, and spies abounded. Except for a small part of its population, it was mostly made up of wanderers, traveling merchants, thieves and fugitives coming from all the kingdoms. The Council made strict laws concerning the Roundabout, as it was called, but hardly ever enforced them. In the end, The Council was nothing more than a puppet government for it too was controlled by Mara. Law and order were her enemies.

One day, shortly after the official opening of the Neutral Zone, the plague sent King Wessex's' wife to her bed; where she quickly succumbed to the fatal, undiscriminating disease. This proved to be too much for King Wessex to accept, so he plunged into a deep depression as would be common when one loses their spouse. Dr. Burgess, the king's doctor, could only watch helplessly, being of little comfort to the family. A heart-broken Darcia, also with nothing she could do, saw her father's condition worsen while Mara put on a mere performance of sorrow, hiding her secret glee, knowing that the King had to hand down his power to her before his passing. Mara the elder was naturally expected to be given this power.

Their Father's illness worsened. His faculties faded with each passing minute. His deterioration tore Darcia apart while Mara remained so calm and cool, secretly calculating her plan to rule the world. Then one day, the sisters were summoned to the King's chamber, and each stood silently on opposite sides of the bed as Dr. Burgess examined the King intently. After a moment, the doctor sighed heavily, and with a kind yet regretful look on his face, addressed the two princesses:

"I'm sorry my ladies, your father has passed."

Mara lifted her head and looked up to the ceiling to let out a slight, undetected smile and sigh of relief even though she wasn't worried about either her sister or Dr. Burgess seeing her jubilation. She had been suppressing it long enough all the while waiting for this day and the coming future that would see her on the throne. Darcia, in stark contrast to her sister's reaction, knelt at his side, taking her father's hand, and kissing it softly, her salty tears falling to the floor. Unlike Mara, she had always dreaded this day's arrival. Darcia kissed her father's forehead and stood up.

As Darcia went to leave the room, Mara stretched her right hand out and asked, "Will you honor our father, and Hagen?" Darcia knew what she wanted from her, a kiss followed by the words, "My Queen." Darcia instead went and stood by her father's side and, as she stroked his forehead, lightly replied with defiance, "Let me be the first to deny you as Queen of Hagen. Those who kiss your hand of deceit will only do so for fear of you, not out of respect for Hagen. That is because one must not demand nor require respect. Only those who lead out of love are worthy. I will not be part of the court of deception you will form. There is nothing you can do or say to sway me because I know you. The rest of the world is about to find out exactly who you are. Those who are obliged, mainly out of fear, to call you *Queen* will be your enemies in their hearts." Darcia put her hand on the King's forehead once more and brushed his hair back lightly. Then she turned to leave the room.

"Whosoever is against the Queen shall die!" Mara shouted out over her father's motionless body. Darcia stopped suddenly and turned to her sister.

"Are you threatening me? Is there any question that if I were to enter the world minutes before you, that you would be the one kneeling this day? Yes, we both know the answer to that," Darcia shot out in such a sarcastic tone that it caused Mara to withdraw her hand. She knew that Darcia would not recognize her as Queen. She was only trying to intimidate her. Just then, two maid servants came into the room, each carrying fresh linens.

"My Queen, the doctor sent us to prepare the King for the ceremony," one of them said as they both knelt before Mara. Darcia stood up and gave her sister a disapproving look as she left the King's bedchamber.

"Do as you were asked, quickly! My Father shall be laid to rest as soon as possible," Mara replied sharply to the servants. She too left the room heading for the Royal guard's quarters located adjacent to the stables. Her personal guards, Keagen, and Bolton met her at the door and, one after the other, knelt and kissed her hand. She looked around first, and then entered the room, closing the door behind her.

"Instruct the crier to announce my father's death and the royal burial tomorrow morning. There will be no festivities proceeding the ceremony. Also, gather the whole court to assemble first thing in the morning. There, I will give them written instructions for the changes I will make pertaining to the laws of Hagen. Also, arrange a council meeting for the following day. I will at that time inform them of the

King's replacement on the Council committee. Also have the court's scribe come to my residence in one hour. I will, at that time, dictate those changes to them. Now, go, do as I command!" Mara demanded as she pointed to the door.

Meanwhile, Darcia, brokenhearted from her father's death, laid on her chamber bed. The night turned stormy. The wind violently caused the trees to dance in chaos. It was relentless, one long heavy gale after another, so strong that she could feel the castle walls vibrating.

Nature was in an uproar, and she understood why. Now with Mara on the throne, not only will the people of Hagen suffer, but the whole earth as well. Darcia stood in front of the open window and lifted her arms slowly. The winds increased in intensity and strength, as if her arms were the conductor's baton directing them to rise according to her will. In one instance she lowered her arms, and the silence was deafening. The trees stood motionless with the wind as an afterthought. Not even a sound of nature's creatures dared to be heard. She turned back into the room, laid back down on her bed, and began to contemplate what she now ought to do.

With her father's death, a large part of her died as well. There have been only two men in her life whom she has loved, her father and Prince Philip of Windermere. She always had a close and wonderful relationship with her father, able to freely show him her love every day. Concerning the prince, she could only love him from afar, for he married Lady Catherine. As the days passed and Mara consolidated her power, it became clear to Darcia that she could have no influence over her sister. Therefore, her presence in the castle was pointless and, quite frankly, she reasoned, too dangerous. Mara was ruthless and ambitious, and Darcia knew that she would stop at nothing to gain power over the world. Surely, she had already begun to scheme. Darcia made up her mind; she would have to leave for a long time, if not forever. Where would she go?

Grimrock

Black Forest

Barrington
Home

n

Hagen

The kingdom of Hagen sat high on a hillside. Grim Rock loomed to the northwest of it and the Black Forest spread out beneath it. Few ever went into the forest. It was a lonely and wild place and most thought it was haunted. Stories of ghosts and people wandering in never to be seen again were spread throughout the land. Parents warned their children not to play too close, much less wander in. Oddly however, from the time she was a child, Darcia had been drawn to it, attracted by the dark, tree-lined paths. Something like a magical, mysterious force seemed to lure her there from the safety of her father's kingdom, calling her to dwell within. No one knew that she often stole away there since she was a child. Now she realized that it was her fate not only to inhabit it, but soon to be its keeper. Now it seemed like the perfect place to hide. Thus, one night under a full moon, Darcia packed a small satchel and headed through a long-forgotten door of the castle toward the Black Forest, her new home.

It wasn't long before Mara learned of her sister's self-imposed exile. At first, she was enraged, but soon thereafter she forgot all about Darcia, as her own plans occupied all her time, plans that were set in motion well before her sister's departure. She set her sights high. She would be no less than an empress. Her plans all hinged on the birth of a boy first and then a girl. She conceived a son by her husband Barrett; she named the boy Brice. Shortly thereafter, she seduced King Phillip and, with his seed planted in her womb, carried the child to its full term, all while skillfully hiding it from all but the royal doctor and a maidservant. It was, for her, nothing more than a fifty-fifty wager, hoping for the birth of a girl, thereby ensuring a blood claim to both thrones.

Now she would soon see if her gamble paid off.

 gut-wrenching scream cut through the midnight darkness of the castle. The maidservant, nodding by the fire, leapt out from a deep sleep. She paused and waited, not sure if she was dreaming. Suddenly, a second, higher-pitched scream was heard, this one calling out for help. The maidservant, Casey, threw the blanket off her and rushed to Queen Mara's room. A third scream filled the corridor as she hurriedly pushed open the heavy wooden door to the Queen's bedchamber. She gasped. Mara was lying in her broad postered bed with her head down and her hands clutching at her stomach. The maidservant held her light closer revealing a large splotch of deep red blood on the sheets. She held her hand to her mouth. The Queen let out another scream.

"Casey! Get Dr. Burgess! hurry!" demanded the Queen as she thrashed back and forth in pain.

"Yes, my Queen," Casey replied. As she turned away and went through the door, she nearly crashed into the man himself. Dr. Burgess had come rushing down the corridor. He was already aware of the Queen's plight and ready to assist. Casey let out a short yelp of surprise.

"Be calm girl!" the doctor snapped. "I need some water and clean dry clothes." The little maid rushed off. "Bring another light, too!" the Doctor called after her.

As Queen Mara rocked back and forth in pain, she thought back to her first birth, her son Brice, just a few short years ago. She was troubled for herself this time, unlike the more pleasant, painless birth of her firstborn. Something was very wrong now and she knew it. She felt like her insides were caught in a whirlpool, spinning inwardly, sucking down not only the baby inside her, but every organ in the vicinity. She felt the baby in distress, but that was secondary to her well-being. Because it was such an arduous and unpleasant pregnancy, it could only be fitting that the birth should go her way; that is, it must produce a healthy daughter! The answer would be only moments away. She gritted her teeth in grim anticipation.

Dr. Burgess came into the Queen's chamber and placed his bag on the bed, quietly evaluating the scene. The Queen was calming herself with visible effort, biting back the pain that was wracking her body. She locked eyes with Dr. Burgess. Grabbing him by the shirt, she pulled him close to her and said in a low, steady voice, "Burgess, there is something wrong with the baby. Help me!"

Burgess pulled the bedding away and lifted the Queen's nightgown. He reached into his bag and removed a small glass bottle. Casey returned with the water, clean rags, and another lantern. Turning the cap on the bottle, the doctor motioned for Casey to hand him a cloth.

Soaking it with the contents of the bottle, he cleaned the area thoroughly with a detached air that only barely covered his own deep agitation.

"Casey, hand me the small knife that is in my bag — and be careful, it is extremely sharp."

Dr. Burgess looked at the Queen as he soaked the cloth once more, this time applying the contents of the bottle to her lower abdomen.

"This will help numb the area," he explained to the Queen. She closed her eyes, anticipating that something more painful was imminent.

He reached for the knife that Casey was holding. "Now you hold the Queen, Casey, and keep her from any sudden movements." The maid servant, her eyes wide as saucers, hurried to fulfill the doctor's orders. She placed her hands firmly on the shoulders of the queen and murmured an apology. Burgess suspected that the cord had found its way around the baby's neck, cutting off its circulation and stifling that first breath that it had yet to even take. Unfortunately, at this moment, there was no way to be sure.

He positioned himself over the bed and made a horizontal incision across the Queen's lower abdomen. He opted to cut lower after determining the baby's position, fully aware of the blood loss that could occur if the delivery should take longer than expected. It was a difficult choice that he was forced to make. Either he could ease the delivery by making surgical incisions which certainly would lead to an uncontrolled blood loss, obviously dangerous and usually fatal for the mother, or he could let the delivery continue naturally, with the risk that both the child and the Queen might perish.

The Queen did not realize that the doctor made a first cut; the topical numbing agent was working quite well. Upon making the second cut, however, she quickly stiffened and then fainted dead away.

"Oh sir, will she be alright?" the maid servant asked with a tremor in her voice. Dr. Burgess said nothing. He was deep in concentration, understanding now that the baby was in serious trouble. Casey did not know what to make of the doctor's silence. She turned back to the Queen and, with a gentle motion, brushed the sweaty locks from her forehead. Burgess had located the cord. He turned the baby's head and gently lifted it, at the same time slowly pulling it by the shoulders.

"Casey," he murmured, "…the clamp and the scissors in my bag, hand them to me! The clamp is upturned at its end, you will see it."

The maidservant shifted her attention away from the Queen with some effort. She quickly removed the instruments and handed them to Dr. Burgess, returning to her place by the queen at once. Dr. Burgess set the clamp first, then cut the cord with a swift, precise movement of his wrist. With a mildly irritated look at the maidservant, he said, "Casey, place clean clothes around the area, and on the bed, here, in front of me. It is dangerous to leave things in such a state." His voice was distracted, and Casey watched with wonder as he casually pulled the baby into the light of the world. She had never seen such a thing. Indeed, her embarrassment at witnessing the queen in such an intimate and vulnerable state was overcome by her awe of the doctor who seemed to do everything without even thinking about it. Little did she know that the doctor too was wracked with anxiety, although he had begun to breathe easier now that the infant was free from any immediate danger. Nonetheless, there was still more to do.

He put the baby gently on the bed next to the queen, who still had not awakened. Next, he pulled out of his bag a long hose and then an object that looked like a balloon. Connecting the balloon to the hose, he placed the open end of the hose into the mouth of the infant and began to squeeze. Suddenly the baby gasped and began to cry heartily. The doctor, greatly relieved, smiled as he removed the tube and started wiping the baby off with a clean cloth. He — for it was a boy, he was squalling loudly, his little face scrunched up with anger at having been so unceremoniously thrust into the world. The doctor motioned Casey over. With gentle hands she lifted the baby and swaddled it in the last of the clean cloth. The cries soon dissipated.

With the baby seemingly stable, the doctor turned his attention back to the Queen. He checked her heart rate and breathing. She was still unconscious. He then began to clean the incisions, sewing the inner one first. Then he cleansed the outside cut, repeating the procedure.

Gradually, the Queen regained consciousness. Her hands surveyed her body, starting with her head and continuing all the way down to her stomach, which was tender to the touch. Still in a daze from the trauma to her body, she lifted her head and saw Casey holding the baby. A weird smile came across her face. It was not one of joy, no, it was a cynical smirk. For months she had to wear the opposite smile, one of feigning joy, as the child occupied her womb. This present smile was more a product of her overarching plot unfolding before her eyes.

The doctor stood by her side and gave her the news, "It's a boy, my Queen!"

Casey held the gently squirming baby out to her, motioning for her to take hold of the child, thinking it would ease and comfort her. The Queen, however, coldly pushed Casey's arm away and turned her head in the opposite direction.

Casey was puzzled. How could the Queen's emotions shift so suddenly? Was she weeping at the sight of the baby? She looked down again at his little face, so serene, now in sleep. He had a thin but abundant crop of golden hair. There was nothing seemingly wrong with the infant, so how could such a joyous occasion be met with tears of despair? Casey wondered. Dr. Burgess caught her eyes with a warning gaze. She stepped back to the corner with the baby still in her arms. Without another word, or even a glance toward the Queen, Dr. Burgess gathered his instruments into his bag and departed from the bedchamber.

The old fool thought the Queen. *How much can he know? How much does he suspect?* It was too early to tell. The wail she had let escape at the sight of her disfigured body was a telltale sign; it was stupid of her to let her deep-seated vanity nearly destroy all she had put into action. The thought of these schemes pushed her despair aside. Her plan was for now thwarted; she still needed a girl to install as Queen of Windemere and then marry her off to Brice, thus uniting the kingdoms and allowing her to rule as regent. Suddenly the pain lessened at the thought of her becoming Queen--no, Empress, of the entire world! There was so much yet to do. With almost a year of planning undone, she would have to try again. A woman of such deception had a pocketful of contingency plans. The one thing that she could never have control over, however, was that of the child's gender. That was one bet she had already lost.

"Casey, go and wake Bolton and Keagan!" the Queen said with a forceful tone. Casey, still holding the newborn, stepped back into the light with only a hint of hesitation. "Tell Keagan to prepare two horses for travel! Bring Bolton to my room! After you have done that, bathe and dress the baby with warm clothing!"

"Y-yes my Queen," Casey replied. She headed down to the guards' quarters which were two floors down from the King's court suite.

Casey's heart raced as she walked down the long corridor leading to the King's Guard's quarters. The walk was too long for her liking. Thoughts of Bolton and Keagan surfaced closer to her memory with each step. Images of that summer night flashed by her eyes like lightning, blinding and fast. It was on a hot night last summer. Barrett and Mara had gone out to the Roundabout for a Council meeting. She always liked walking in the castle's lower quad courtyard where it was cooler during the summer months. She turned a corner and there they were, soaked in drink, sitting outside their quarters. They both wreaked of alcohol.

"Good evening, Miss Casey. What brings you out at this hour?" Bolton asked, surprised to see her passing by. Keagan sprang up off the bench that he was lying on. Bolton's speech was noticeably slurred.

"I could not sleep due to the heat, this year has been unusually hot," she replied as she started to walk faster, sensing trouble. The two of them gave each other a wink and a nod. Each grabbed one of her arms and jerked her backwards.

"What's your rush? Sit! Have a drink, and let's get to know one another," Keagan said and pulled her by the hand downward, causing her to fall onto one knee. Bolton, the stronger of the two, put his hand under her chin and lifted her head up. By now Keagan, a short, stout, heavyset brute, positioned himself behind her, leaving her no way to wiggle free.

"Please! No! I must go because my lady will be back tomorrow, and I have to see that everything is in order." Just then Bolton, in one motion, tore her summer dress right down the middle. Casey was not wearing any under garments due to the heat. Keagan smiled as he stood over her. She was lying in the fetal position on the ground, crying. He grabbed her by the legs and stretched them open.

"You just relax, Miss Casey. You may enjoy this. I know I will," Bolton promised as he removed his lower garment, exposing himself.

"You can scream but no one will hear it. In fact, there is no one here to guard now that the King's court is on the journey to the Neutral Zone. It is just us and a few castle-keepers. They dare not interfere with the King's Knights."

Just as Keagan was busy removing his sword and belt, Casey suddenly and easily brought the big man to the ground with a swift knee to the groin. She pulled her dress to cover herself as best she could and ran towards the service quarters. Keagan, with his head spinning from the drink, laughed uncontrollably, watching his fellow assailant fall to the ground, grasping his midsection.

"Get that bitch!" Bolton screamed as he gasped for air.

"Let her go, it's a much smaller world now," she heard Keagan say from behind as she hurried away. "Won't be long and our paths will cross again. Next time, less drink and more Casey! We will have another crack at her soon enough," Keagan said, reaching for a bottle on the bench where he was lying.

Bolton, whose pride, and manhood was just dealt a huge blow, rose to his feet, hunched over, and replied, "Sooner the better. She needs to be taught some manners."

Now, Casey had to face them again. She knew they wouldn't have time to get their revenge on her because they had to obey the Queen and nothing more. Casey made her way down that all-too-familiar spiral staircase towards the guard's quarters. As she approached the doorway, Bolton surprised her by grabbing her arm and pulling her slowly into the room.

"Look what the gods have provided us, my comrades… a virgin for the night's festivities."

Casey, pulling her arm loose, stepping back towards the door, and looking at Keagan, said, "You are to prepare two horses for travel." She then turned to Bolton to inform him, "And you are to go to the Queen's chambers immediately. I have never seen her, in all my years at her beckoning call, so distraught. Believe me, she is not in the mood for your plots and schemes."

Bolton and Keagan both grabbed their swords and belts and grudgingly headed through the doorway. Bolton stopped, looked at Casey and said, "The next time I see you, I will see all of you, and take the flower that you are so unwilling to surrender to a man."

When Bolton entered the room, The Queen was sitting up in her bed. It became obvious by her countenance that she was still in great pain and agitation. Bolton stood by the side of the bed. The Queen was sipping from a cup. Just then Casey entered the room holding the infant. He was wrapped in a thick blanket and a bonnet had been placed on his head. Bolton was not surprised to see Casey holding the child, for although Mara convinced herself she was careful in not revealing her condition for the last eight months or so, some did manage to find out, yet remain quiet. "Put the child in the crib and leave us," Mara said in a commanding tone to Casey. Casey placed the boy in the crib, covered him with a blanket and brushed his hair back lightly; finally, she kissed his forehead and left the room. She sensed that the child was in danger.

Standing by, she put her ear close to the thick wooden door in hope that she could hear their conversation.

Mara pointed to the child as she looked at Bolton and said, "You and Keagan are to take that child deep into the woods, beyond Grim Rock. There you are to place the child on the ground and place heavy stones on it. Make sure that not a glimmer of light peers through. Then, stay there until you hear nature bemoaning. Upon the child's death, the earth will shudder and cry. The walking beasts and animals of all kinds will groan in pain. The full moon will hold back its light until dawn." Mara turned and looked out of her window. "Every living soul will be awakened by this and be in fear. Those who are waiting for the "ONE" to bring unity throughout the world will be lost tonight; all hope will die along with this bastard," Mara said vindictively. She turned back and continued giving him her explicit instructions:

"After your return, you are to seek out the doctor. Upon finding him you are to bring him to Devil's Cliff where you will throw him off. The old fool will never see it coming; he has been blind to everything from the beginning of my pregnancy. I need to have this secret fall a few hundred feet to its death along with him. Now go, do as I require!"

Mara called out for Casey to come in. Casey paused, allowing sufficient response time to not let the Queen suspect that she may have been right outside eavesdropping. She opened the door and Mara pointed to the child and said, "Give the child to Bolton!" Casey handed the baby over to Bolton. In her mind, she hoped that they would fail somehow, thus saving the child and sealing their fate as well. Bolton handled the baby indifferently, like a parcel or sack of grain. The child made no noise despite the guard's reckless handling. Bolton made his way out of the Queen's chamber and down the hall to the stairwell.

Casey now turned her attention to the Queen's discomfort; she tossed the pillows behind Mara's head in turn avoiding any eye contact with her. As she began to change the bed linens, she could feel the Queen staring at her. It gave her a most uncomfortable feeling, as if the Queen was seeking to discover her soul's intentions. The Queen lifted herself up slowly against the headboard.

"Casey," she began, "are you not a loyal subject of the Kingdom of Hagen? Upon your decision to choose this as your home, were you aware of my father's desire to rule as he believed would be best for all, even if it meant the sacrifice of one, or a few? Surely you must understand that *ONE* could cause more turmoil and unrest than thousands, given the right circumstances. That *ONE* could even shatter the thin, fragile peace that exists between us and Windermere. Certainly, difficult decisions must be made to preserve this peace. These decisions should be in the hands of those who are strong in will and able to see into the future, those who provide stability and calm thereby avoiding uncontrollable chaos. My father placed a certain degree of trust in you. Now, currently, I need you to strengthen that trust. I need to hear from you that your loyalty to the throne is unwavering, unmovable, no matter what decision or circumstance." Mara was setting her up, playing an emotional game with the young maidservant.

Casey looked down at the floor to break away from the stares of the Queen. She knew what the Queen was asking. She also knew her response would determine whether she would wake up the next morning, or even make it through this day alive. Her answer had to be, at once, disingenuous, and convincing. Casey was accustomed to only speak from the heart and it was simply against her nature to deceive others. Was this a fault that would prove fatal?

"My Queen, I am merely a servant, loyal, scant in education and life's wisdom. I have chosen to serve by my own free will. You and your father have always treated me with respect. Although I am expendable, you have provided shelter, food, and protection. There is absolutely nothing that could undermine my loyalty, cause me to question or doubt the Kingdom's decisions. My life is given over to thee with no expectation of reward or acknowledgement. I rightly serve the Kingdom of Hagen." Casey answered as best she could but was doubtful the Queen believed a word she spoke.

The Queen tilted her head and looked at Casey. Without looking up, Casey could feel the probing stare, causing her to feel an uncomfortable prickly sensation. It was a power play on Mara's part. She was a master of mind games. However, the young maid rose to the occasion, remade eye contact, and the two were locked into a game of "who would blink first". As their eyes met, the Queen raised her head up and smiled, saying, "I do believe you are loyal, my young maidservant. I have watched you carefully these past months while I carried the child. I have seen your concern for me as well as the child. And now, you just have me to focus on. I am going to get some sleep. Wake me in two hours. I want to make sure I hear nature's cry throughout the land validating the death of *hope*."

Casey took a basin of hand-water and some soiled clothes and headed out of the Queen's bedchamber. Once out of the Queen's sight, she hurried her pace down the stairs and into the servants' quarters. She placed the basin and clothes on a table by the door. As she did this, she heard horses in the courtyard. Looking, she saw Bolton and Keagan with the infant tucked in a basket that was tied around Keagan's waist. Casey put her hands to the glass and hopelessly watched as they faded out of sight.

"You know, this wasn't the original plan for the child. in fact, it was the total opposite." Casey turned to see Dr. Burgess behind her. His hands were clenching his bag to his chest. He was obviously very nervous. He took her by the arm and guided her into an alcove in the hallway and sat her on the window ledge.

"Her own husband had no knowledge of her pregnancy." Casey looked at the doctor in disbelief. He placed his bag on the floor and, looking out the window, explained, "She is a gifted woman when it comes to deception. You must have seen the signs of the charade, being so close to her for these last eight months… covering up her body with long clothes, acting as if she didn't feel well to avoid her husband, intimately.

"Her plan was to have a girl child by King Philip of Windemere. That way, both her son Brice and this latest arrival would be heirs and have her royal blood. She would then wed them together while she, herself, would rule as regent. Sometime later, she would kill her husband off and turn the Kingdom over to her first son, Brice, thus securing Windermere's throne through the new princess. Of course, the problem was that she needed a daughter. Ironically, that has not occurred, as you have seen."

"Wait, you mean to tell me that you knew of this and told no one?" Casey was getting visibly upset as she stood up and confronted the doctor. He disregarded not only her question, but her demeanor as well and continued.

"The one unknown, uncontrollable factor was that of the child's gender; she gambled and lost. Another son would only serve to foil her designs. The child must not live because he has a claim to not only the Kingdom of Windermere, but Hagen as well." Dr. Burgess, spooked by a sound in the distance, checked the corridor in both directions.

"We must try to save this boy," Casey said as she processed all of what the doctor had just revealed to her.

He turned to her and asked, "Why? Who would believe he is heir of two thrones, let alone one? What proof do we have? The testimony of an old barefoot doctor or a maidservant? A would-be king who cannot speak, nourish himself, nor provide shelter? Who would be his subjects?" The doctor was shaking his head frantically.

"Are you afraid of her? Well, I am not! You helped bring this child into the world. Why? To die at the hands of his mother?" Casey's face, in comparison to the doctor's, turned beet red in anger. His, on the other hand, remained as pale as a sheet. She was inflamed as she realized that Dr. Burgess would have the child's blood on his hands in more ways than one.

"Why, you need to ask? Because it is an innocent child! If you require another reason than that, well, I pity you." She glared into the doctor's eyes and in an instant, he broke down in tears.

"You are right, I am an accomplice, a complicit party for aiding the Queen."

"You have a choice now, doctor, you can help right this wrong." Casey softened her tone and put her hands on his shoulders.

"I have an idea," the doctor said. "I know of people who may be able to help. If I give you their identity, you must swear to tell no one. For if you did, you'd put many lives in danger including yours, mine, and the child. If you are suspected in the least, Queen Mara will torture you until you confess everything."

"I promise. I will do anything to save the child," Casey said as convincingly as she knew how.

"I will tell you how you can help; but first, repeat this oath: I swear by all that's dear to me, to keep The Society secret."

Casey dutifully and without hesitation recited it.

Dr. Burgess went on, "Good. I will report to The Society what I have heard. To no one else let slip a word of this."

Casey had no trouble keeping her mouth shut. She had lots of experience looking the other way as the Queen's chamber maid. Indeed, she has personally witnessed more than enough of the Queen's mischief and intrigue.

Dr. Burgess concluded the oath, "I will report with my last breath, faithful, though I will be faced with death." At the word "death" the doctor looked deeply into Casey's eyes searching for any sign of hesitation, simultaneously relaying the seriousness of the situation they were now mutually embroiled in.

Casey drew in a sharp deep breath. She was relieved that others were observing the Queen's evil too yet scared that she is now obligated to snitch on the Queen. Would this, in fact, put her very life in danger?

"I will report with my last breath, faithful, though I will be faced with death," Casey firmly recited, staring right back into Dr. Burgess' eyes.

"Good!" Dr. Burgess hurriedly went on to further explain things. "There is a group of us, a secret society, made up of about three dozen men and women. We are in both Hagen, Windermere, the Neutral Zone, and some of the villages. I can't tell you everything right now, nor can I mention specific names. There are some who are everyday tradesmen, and others in high positions. We must get word to one of them about the child's fate." The doctor had reversed his feelings towards the child because of the guilt caused by Casey's words and now sounded purposeful and genuine in his concern. He picked up his bag and, grabbing Casey's hand, they both made their way down the back stairway to the kitchen.

"Poppel, Poppel!" Dr. Burgess whispered as he slowly opened one of the doors from the kitchen.

"Dr. Burgess, is that you?" A voice came from the darkened room.

"Yes, please get dressed and come out here immediately," he said as he closed the door and turned to Casey.

"Give him a minute, I have an idea." Soon thereafter, a short red-headed boy emerged from the room. Dr. Burgess put his hands to his lips signaling Poppel to be quiet.

"We need to send a message to Mr. Z. Afterwards, do not return here but stay at Mr. Z's until you hear from me and me only," the doctor said to the young man as he grabbed a piece of paper and a writing instrument off a nearby countertop. He then feverishly scribbled down a short message on the paper and folded it. Now he put his hand on one of Poppel's shoulders, tucked the note in one of his pockets, and shoved him lightly to the stairwell as he whispered, "Now go!" Poppel looked at the doctor's face and could tell it was a serious matter. He ran to the stable and in less than a minute rode out, heading for the Roundabout.

The doctor turned his attention back to Casey, "I must check on the Queen. You need to act as normal as possible also. The Queen mustn't sense that anything is going on. It is out of our hands. If we were to leave, she would know we were up to something. All we can do is wait to see when Bolton and Keagan return."

The doctor headed back upstairs as Casey turned towards her chamber to go lay down because of emotional exhaustion. He did turn back in Casey's direction and said with a half grin, "Just pray the boy can stay on the horse!"

oppel managed to reach the outer end of the Neutral Zone. Surrounding it, stood a tall wall which was covered halfway up with vines and thorn bristles. It had separate knee-high walls on both sides, used by guards to keep watch over the perimeter. The overall height gave them the advantage should there be an attempted attack on the Neutral Zone. As Poppel approached, one of the large iron gates swung open. The timing was perfect; he never lost a stride. As he passed through, he gave a wave and a nod to the gatekeeper who ignored him because he was half-asleep. The hour was late. Poppel headed straight for The Toy Box which was owned by Mr. Zimmerman (Mr. Z, as he was known by his friends and patrons). It was the largest shop in the Roundabout, operated by him and his only child, Jill. One side was the store itself with a large storefront window; directly behind it was a large workshop/storage room. On the opposite end was their residence: two bedrooms, a large kitchen in the back, and an even larger living room in the front.

Outside, Poppel tied his horse to a post and stumbled up the stairs. He looked left and right to see if anyone was watching. He then knocked on the door lightly.

"Mr. Z, it's me, Poppel," he said in a low voice as he nervously kept looking around. Mr. Z opened the door. He was a tall, slender gentleman with a mustache and short black hair. He held a tobacco pipe in his hand.

"Poppel, what are you doing here?" Mr. Z asked. He sensed that Poppel was very tense and nervous as he watched him looking from side to side. He gently grabbed Poppel's arm and pulled him in the store slowly. He motioned for Poppel to sit in a chair by the woodstove in the corner of the store. Poppel first looked out the window, back and forth, up and down the street, and then he sat down slowly into the chair. He noticed a heavy odor as his eyes immediately began to water. There was a dense odor of varnish or paint in the air. Mr. Z placed his hand on Poppel's right shoulder.

"Tell me, Poppel, what is wrong. Why are you here and in such a frantic state?" Mr. Z queried, impatiently waiting for the reply.

"Dr. Burgess sent me here to see you," he answered as he reached into his pocket. "He asked me to give you this note." Poppel handed him the note and at once let out a hearty sigh of relief as if to say, "mission accomplished".

"What is this about?" Mr. Z asked as he took it from Poppel.

"I don't know, sir. The doctor didn't say why but just that I make haste to get here."

Mr. Z sat back in his chair and unfolded the note. He wanted to respect the doctor's wishes of privacy, which in turn would protect Poppel from any knowledge of its contents. Therefore, he read it to himself. It said:

"It is of great urgency that you send members to the bottom of Grim Rock and intercept Mara's guards who have a newborn boy in their possession. Overcome them, secure the baby, and provide a refuge for it! You must hurry, before it is too late!"

At the bottom of the note there was the valid insignia that Mr. Z recognized as proof that its sender belonged to the Society. Mr. Z sprang up out of his chair. "Alright Poppel, you must get back to the castle quickly before the Queen knows you are missing," he commanded as he grabbed a coat from a closet near the shop's door.

"I was told to stay here by Dr. Burgess," Poppel answered as he stood up rubbing his eyes.

"Please, you must return. Mara will grow very suspicious if you are found to be missing. Trust me; go back at once!"

"But sir, what is this all about? Why so much secrecy?" The red-headed courier asked, so perplexed by all of this.

"Son, you need not know. It is for your own safety. You are in enough danger. I'm sorry, you must go now!" Poppel let out a reluctant sigh.

Mr. Z immediately threw a coat on and hurried out the door in the direction of Pete's Tavern. He walked briskly, almost at a jogging pace. Reaching the door, he opened it and scanned the entire bar. There at the far end was Tippet, a groundskeeper by trade for the Neutral Zone. He had a pint of watered-down hops that the innkeeper called "beer". Oftentimes on his days off, well, every day that he had off, one would find him there, and sitting next to JD when the troupe was in town. Mr. Z tapped the man on the shoulder and waited for him to turn around to confirm that he was Tippet. He nodded his head towards the front door and began to walk out of the tavern, as he threw a coin on the bar for Tippet's tab.

Mr. Z headed for the alley next to the tavern with Tippet lagging just a few steps behind him. The two stopped and faced one another. Tippet's much taller and broader shoulders cast a big shadow over the lanky Mr. Z. He laid a hand on Tippet's right shoulder and, with a distressed look, said to him, "We are needed. There is a newborn child in jeopardy! At this very moment the Queen's guards are headed into the forest to the foot of Grim Rock where they are going to kill the child on Mara's orders. This is all I know. There is no time to guess her motives or who this child is. We don't have any time for details or a plan. You must intercept them! Stop at the Fullerton's and see if Nate and his elder brother are home. Get whatever you need for weapons… Rope, farm tools, anything to help overcome the guards. Rescue that child and bring it here!" The two men hurried back towards the front of the tavern where Tippet's horse was standing. Tippet untied his horse, mounted, and headed in the direction of the Fullerton's home.

eanwhile, Keegan and Bolton, with the child, pushed deeper into Black Forest. Piercing up through the mushroom-like treetops loomed Grim Rock. Neither one of them had spoken a word since they left Hagen. Their silence was only broken by the sounds of the horses' hooves. The trail that they were on ended over a mile ago. They found themselves weaving and dodging thorn-covered branches and serpentine along the mountain's steep base. It was thought that no one ever dared to wander so deep into this forest. The trees were magnificently high. The tops of them touched one another, like pieces of a puzzle interlocked, thus giving the forest its name. The light from the sun or moon would penetrate tiny holes in the mushroom-like tops, creating pinpointed beams of light. Without those tiny beams of light, the two men would have needed lanterns to reach their destination. The forest's root system became more exposed the higher they traveled up the rock's base. It would be easy for one of their horses to slip on the moss-covered roots and perhaps twist an ankle, leaving them incapable of riding any further. Even the bravest of men would be just a bit nervous in this environ-ment. Bolton was no exception. He was a rational man, but anyone could become fearful given the right circumstances.

Unfortunately for Bolton, his counterpart was a very weak man when it came to dealing with the unknown. The air was getting thinner and noticeably colder. The horses were breathing heavily, and their hooves were hitting the ground like a hammer on an anvil, a sign that they were laboring to get a good deep breath of air.

"This is far enough Bolton. No one will ever come up this far under these conditions," Keagan said with a distressed look on his face.

"That's the whole idea you moron!" Bolton turned to Keagan and gave him a sarcastic sneer. "Another hundred yards — I'm not leaving anything to chance. She will kill us if we fail!"

As they continued, the beams of light coming through the treetops turned red in color. Keagan stretched out one of his hands, the light turning his skin to a dull crimson. A sense of panic came over him. He noticed there were no more sounds of nature: no birds, owls or anything that would signify life aside from them. He saw that there was no vegetation up this high, not even any moss left to cover over the roots of trees. He listened intently, trying to hear any other sign of life.

Just then, a strong breeze blew, coming directly in front of the two of them. Keagan took it as a good sign. It was nature in movement. He knew that when there was wind, it meant that a change was coming. As the incline increased, the force of wind intensified considerably, making it difficult for the men to catch their breath in the thinning air.

Bolton turned to him and said, "Untie the basket for me, this is far enough." Keagan could hear a hint of fear in Bolton's voice. He wondered if the change in light and wind was the reason for his partner's abrupt decision to stop and dismount. He jumped down, reached up for the rope, and untied the basket from Bolton's saddle.

They took the baby and put him on the ground. As the baby touched the earth, a bright blue light, with what seemed like a silhouette of a figure in the middle of it, suddenly shone on the path just a couple of hundred feet ahead of them. The red light that pierced through the treetops minutes ago had vanished and yielded to the blue light approaching them.

"Hurry, get as many boulders as you can! Cover the child and let's get out of here!" Bolton shouted out, clearly distraught by the light that was now approaching them. Keagan never took his eyes off the oncoming bluish hue. He felt around with his boots and, in doing so, found a couple of small rocks. He quickly bent down, and without looking, placed them beside the child's head.

Now, they both stopped and stood motionless as the light moved directly in front of them. In the center of the light, they saw the figure of a woman. She was wearing a white cape and, under it, a white silk dress that caressed her breasts perfectly. The dress had a laced border around the v-cut neck and at the end of the sleeves. There was a crystal hanging down from her neck that shined like a prism with all the colors of the rainbow reflecting out from it. Her lips were rose colored, moist, and shiny. Her eyes looked black with eyeshadow to match. Black raven hair with wavy curls rippled down her shoulders like ocean waves until they reached the shores of her breasts.

The wind calmed and the scent of her perfume filled their senses. The two men stood dumbfounded and mesmerized by her beauty. They didn't realize, or care for that matter, but they were undone.

"Do you know who I am?" The woman asked the two of them, floating closer to them. Her voice was melodious but strong. She was dressed all in white, a sign of purity and innocence. She Intended to convey a message to the two of them with the helpless child at their feet.

Bolton looked at the ground and mumbled, "No" he responded. He felt like a child in her presence and no longer in control. Keagen watched him in unbelief. He couldn't believe his eyes as he watched his accomplice turn into the woman's subordinate.

Darcia (for that was who she was) stepped right in front of him and replied, "I am the Keeper of the Forest and the Protector of all who enter it! What are you doing here?" Before they could answer her eyes locked onto the baby at their feet, "What have we here?" She bent down, slid both her hands under the baby, and lifted him up off the cold, moist ground. Fortunately, he was still wrapped in the blanket.

"What have we got here? she said again. Such a handsome child. What have you two to do with him?" Darcia asked without making eye contact with either of the guards.

Mara's henchmen gave no response. They were frozen in fear of what the seductive woman was going to do to them. She arrived just in time before they had a chance to drop a single stone on top the baby.

Darcia then looked around from side to side and said, "I know you two are not lost. I have watched you come through the forest many times in search of accused traitors and criminals fleeing from Hagen. Did you ever wonder why you were never successful in the capture of even one?"

"How... how do you know this?" stuttered Keagan.

She proudly responded, "This is my domain gentlemen. Nothing happens here that I don't know about!" Darcia began to slowly rock the child in her arms while looking down at him. She had a knowing grin on her face as she then glanced back up at the two would-be assassins.

Now, if you will both allow me to explain your present situation: "You are pawns, carrying out my sister's schemes." Darcia looked Bolton directly in the eyes and asked, "Do you have any children?"

"N-no. No, I d-do not." Bolton was the one stuttering now, having a hunch she already knew the answer. She then turned to Keagan and asked the same question.

"I-I do not." He said with a quivering voice. He was in fear for his life. The question deepened that fear as he wondered where this line of questioning was headed. He had an urge to run, but his boots felt glued to the ground. He realized that they were in trouble and decided to try pleading his case, "Your sister gave us orders to bring the child here. We had no choice; she would kill us if we disobeyed her. She has killed dozens of other subjects for less."

Bolton looked at his spineless accomplice and shook his head at the futility of Keagan's desperate plea.

Darcia continued, "You should be worrying about me, the "good" sister. She meant for you to take the life of this child, but I am going to exact the same punishment on both of you in a slightly different way. It shall not be by physical death as you were about to inflict." She cradled the baby in one arm as she reached into one of her dress pockets and presented a small leather satchel. She carefully untied the pouch and poured its contents into the palm of her other hand.

Looking at the two of them she said, "I am a simple witch. I like to get right to it. Don't worry, you won't feel a thing." The two guards stood there motionless.

Bolton was thinking he could grab his sword and take her by surprise; he began to inch his right hand across his waist. Keagan, seeing this, gave him a stern, defiant look of disapproval and cleared his throat. Darcia could see what Bolton was about to attempt and so she took a step closer to them, taunting him, daring him even. His hand froze in the air, and he sharply and audibly inhaled.

"I filled this satchel full of a potent — perhaps a bad choice of words — blend of special ingredients. I believe it is a fitting recipe for this occasion. I am going to see to it that neither of you will ever bring forth life from your loins. Close your eyes, take a deep breath, and listen to my words." She then raised the powder up before them, blew into her palm which lifted the light substance into the air in front of their faces, and while they inhaled it, she recited this spell:

"How dare you harm the meek?
Raging with your fire!
Your sword will be too weak
to take what you desire.

Do you reach for her red hair,
Sparkling in the sun?
Touch her only if you dare
You cursed, unlucky one!

When you would seek to conquer,
You're but a wing on a moth
You're but a dog's whimper
You lust, but you are soft!"

Their eyes began to water immediately as a trance-like state came upon them. Darcia watched, and seeing their reactions, she had no doubt that the spell took effect. Darcia turned to the two immoral, and now impotent, guards and addressed them as if they were children.

"Alright, you two run back to your Queen. My nephew and I are going to spend some time getting acquainted. Do give my regards to my sister!" She turned with the baby in hand, and they faded from their sight just as she appeared to them, surrounded by the bright, blue light.

Bolton and Keagan looked at one another without saying a word. They hastily got on their horses and started back in the direction of Hagen.

hile in transport somewhere deep in the forest, Darcia stopped for a moment, looked at the infant sleeping comfortably in her arms, and said, "You are going to be a world-changer when I am done with you, little man. I will see that no harm shall come to you, though some things must come to pass, for fate cannot be bargained with or controlled." She sighed, and, waving her hand, chanted:

"To your mother you were a thorn
on the day that you were born
Blood of my blood, I'm providing
the critical gift of magical hiding

Building trust through innocence
Melting the ice of vigilance
You will free with comedy
Those who are trapped in treachery

Your true identity will come to light
and those who thirst for a better life
Will cheer you on as you ascend
And in love and honor, all knees will bend"

Darcia headed to a house on the farthest edge of the forest that was in a village called Clearwater. It sat on the side of a small pond at the mouth of Crystal River. She came to the door and knocked lightly. Opening the door was a slender woman. A stranger, upon meeting her for the first time might think she was sickly. She was tall, with rose-colored, sunken cheekbones, and thinning hair. Not an ounce of fat was found on her, yet she had the strength of a team of horses. She got that way from her upbringing on her parent's farm, one that flourished and was well-known throughout the villages, providing food for the plague-stricken land.

"Hello Sandra, do you remember me?" Darcia asked as she turned her head downward towards the infant and grinned.

"Yes, of course. You are Darcia, the Keeper of the Forest." she replied.

"Please dear, we can skip right over the formalities. May I come in?"

"Yes, please do. Come in. Sit. My husband should be back shortly if you would rather speak with the two of us," she said. Darcia entered the humble home. There was a small kitchen in the back corner, a large bed on the opposite end, and a round table and chairs. It was spotless. A smell of fresh bread was in the air. Darcia stood in the kitchen area and replied,

"Interesting, it's like you are reading my mind, I do need to talk to the two of you," Darcia said. Sandra came closer to get a better view of the child.

"What a beautiful baby! Is he yours?" Sandra dared to ask with her eyes all lit up.

"No, but you are close. Good guess, anyways." replied Darcia. She then opened the blanket fully, lifted the child up and presented him to Sandra.

"Would you like to hold him?" Darcia asked, already knowing the answer, as Sandra took the child from her as naturally as if she were his own mother. She cradled him as she kissed his cheek. A tear escaped one of her eyes as her heart melted from the beauty of the child in her arms. She was taken aback by the special connection she instantly began to feel.

"His eyes are glued to you Sandra. Something about you is special to him. May I ask if you have any goats' or cows' milk? I have traveled long and far and have not yet had a chance to feed or bathe him." Darcia explained.

"Of course, we can feed him. By then Benjamin will be home. He can keep you company while I bathe him.",

Sandra fetched the milk and poured some in a new leather pouch made by her husband for his homebrew that he would cook up in the shed out back. She sat, with the infant, at the table in the kitchen area. Darcia watched Sandra's every move. She watched Sandra tenderly hold the child as if he was her very own son. How attentive she was to his every movement, looking for clues to learn as only a mother could.

Right then, the front door opened slowly as Benjamin came in carrying a bag and his jacket.

"Look honey, look what I'm holding." Sandra couldn't wait to show Benjamin the baby.

Ben, as his wife always called him, immediately dropped the bag, almost on his toes. He went by her side and smiled, "What a handsome young man. His eyes are captivating, I can see a long line of broken hearts floating in the wake behind him. Oh, excuse my manners Darcia, I didn't see you there." Ben said as he held the baby's tiny fragile fingers.

"I wouldn't have it any other way Benjamin! I too was taken when I first laid eyes on the child. There is no denying that there is something special about him. He lights up the room naturally... runs in the family." Darcia jokes.

"Whose child, is he? What is his name and why did you come to Clearwater with him?" Ben asked. He was a very practical man. He liked to take things apart, see how they worked and how they're made, making him seem a bit too blunt. He didn't mean to be rude by not giving Darcia a chance to answer each question separately.

"Well Benjamin, why don't you help Sandra tend to the baby? We have traveled a few hours to get here. A fresh swaddling blanket and a warm bath would be good for the child", Darcia suggested instead, evading all his questions. Nonetheless, Sandra was way ahead of the request, having a pot of warm water, a bar of ash soap, and clean linen ready on the other side of the room on their bed. Ben took the child from her arms and gazed into his eyes intently, as if he was trying to look into the child's soul. The baby let out a little squeak and seemed to stare back at him. "He likes me!" Ben felt his heart melt.

Sandra poured the water into a large metal tub that she used for crushing fruit for her preserves. She poured some colder water in, mixing it back and forth, finding the right temperature. "Alright honey, bring him over here and hold him in the basin."

Ben did as his wife had asked and she gently washed the child from head to toe. She began to hum a song that her own mother sang to her as an infant while she was being bathed. The couple looked at one another. Sandra had a tear escaping from one eye. Ben nodded his head up and down, knowing what his wife was thinking and feeling.

Darcia responded to the moment, "I remember how the three of us met that day on the edge of the forest, not too far from here. It was a trying time for you two as I recall, both physically and emotionally. I felt that I was of little comfort to you since you had carried your child for so many weeks only to have fate change its fickle mind. If I may ask, is your situation the same? Are you two still trying to start a family?" The two of them looked at one another, then back to Darcia, and nodded their heads quickly up and down. "Yes, yet, the doctor says we shouldn't get our hopes too high due to the damage done at that time — and the number of other times," Ben painfully recalled as he stroked Sarah's hair. They were not used to discussing this deep pain with anyone.

Darcia finally revealed, "This child is *very* close to me. His mother is also, but, in a different sense. I don't mean to be so vague, but what I am about to tell you can't leave this home," Darcia paused so they understood the seriousness of what she was about to tell them. "This baby was abandoned, given up by his mother, and left to die. You will, in time, learn of this woman. For now, I must keep you in the dark concerning the people and events surrounding this boy. As you can see, I rescued him, but it is not possible for me to raise him, so I am looking for the two best parents I can find for this special boy." Darcia paused again and then delivered the good news, "I want you two to take this baby and nurture him as your own."

Ben and Sandra stared back at Darcia, speechless and stunned by this amazing news.

Darcia went on, "People will ask you how it is possible that you suddenly have a baby. You will explain that the two of you kept it a secret because of Sandra's previous miscarriage a year ago. There will be those who will doubt that the child is yours, but you must continue to claim that he is your own and push back on the prying of some into your personal life. This is my only request."

"What do you think Ben? Can we keep him? Couldn't we pretend that he is ours?" Sandra turned to her husband, knowing that he would have the final say.

Ben responded to Sara's upturned face, noticing the tear still on her cheek, and softly replied, "Nothing would make me happier! We will have a son, and we will not have to pretend!"

Darcia was pleased to see their positive response. She went on, "In raising this child you will ensure that a special boy will carry on to his proper place in this world. You will not be alone in caring for him. I will be there helping, watching, and protecting him, where I can. Meanwhile, you must act normal, be yourselves, be the parents that you know in your hearts you can be." Darcia pulled her shawl up higher on her shoulders as she kissed the child on the cheek and headed towards the front door. She turned back to them and proclaimed, "By the way, I named him Jack!" Darcia then smiled and closed the door behind her, leaving the two new parents stunned but overjoyed.

n the meantime, Keegan and Bolton rode silently side by side on the widening trail, both lost in troubled thoughts on how to explain to the Queen why the child is still alive. They each knew very well that failure was totally unacceptable, and which carried unthinkable consequences.

"What are we going to tell her, Bolton?" wondered Keagan, breaking the silence between the two of them.

"It's pretty simple," Bolton said as he pulled back on the reins and stopped. "We are going to have to convince her that we did indeed carry out her orders. To fool her, we both must have the same story. Do you understand?"

Keagan stopped and turned his horse towards him and said, "We must tell her the truth! Her sister ambushed us, put us under a spell that froze us, then took the child and disappeared into the darkness. After her spell wore off, we made haste to get reinforcements and pursue the witch. What is wrong with that story?"

"No, we have to lie!" Bolton was visibly frustrated. "She will kill us if we fail her. We need to get our story straight. We are in this together. Don't you see why she sent both of us? ...to trip one of us in a lie, contradicting one another. Apart, we will die! Together, we have a better chance of saving ourselves."

"She will know we are lying; she will look right through us." Keagan reiterated his position, and it was evident that he was firm in his plan. "We have better odds just telling her that Darcia took the child. At least it is the truth."

"There's one thing wrong with your story; the child isn't dead. Remember what she said? If we fail, we will experience a death not yet seen in this world!" Bolton couldn't believe how stupid Keagan was. "Your story screams failure. With mine, at least we have a chance to buy some time, time to search for him." Bolton replied.

Keagan grudgingly nodded his head affirmatively and the two of them headed towards Hagen, seemingly both in agreement on the plan.

The sun was just rising as they approached the castle gates. The outer gate first and, soon after, the inner one, began to lift when they were about thirty yards away. As the two of them passed through the gates, Keagen looked up and could see the light of the morning sun dimly through the "murder holes" above him. For a second, he swore he could see Mara above, rock in hand, arm cocked, waiting to pelt them. They dismounted and headed straight for the Queen's bedchamber. The castle was eerily quiet. Reaching the staircase, Bolton grabbed Keagan's arm.

"Let me do the talking! Keep your answers to one word! We did as she ordered, went deep into the woods, placed the child on the ground, covered it high with rocks, and left it to die. Nothing more, do not offer anything more!" Bolton released his arm and tapped lightly on the Queen's door as he pushed it open slowly.

The Queen was sitting upright in her bed. The guards stood in the doorway waiting for her to acknowledge their presence. She had fresh clothes on, and her hair was up. On the table next to her bed was a pitcher of water and a plate with bread and some fruit. She gave out a slight moan as she sat up higher and waved her hand, motioning them to enter the room.

"Why did I not hear nature's cry? Did you not do as I ordered?" the Queen asked with suspicion in her voice.

The two guards bowed deeply. "We did exactly as you ordered. We went deeper into the Forest than any other, placed the baby on the cold ground, gathered rocks, placed them atop of him, and then returned immediately. We were not seen by anyone. The child is dead." Bolton declared as he looked straight into the Queen's eyes, never breaking eye contact. He stood waiting for the Queen's response.

"The doctor gave me something to help me sleep," Mara replied slowly as she rubbed her forehead, drowsy from the medicine. "That may be why I did not hear nature's bemoaning of the infant's fate." Mara began to position herself on the edge of the bed in an attempt to stand. Bolton went to her aid, but she shunned his hand away and stood up holding the bed post to steady herself. "Now we must deal with the witnesses; I speak of Casey and the doctor. He is downstairs in his office. Go there at once! Grab some of the medicine that he uses to put his patients to sleep before he performs surgical procedures on them. Render him helpless with his own medicine. Be sure you are not seen; if you are, we will just make the list of witnesses longer and deal with them in a like manner. Take him to Devil's Cliff. Be sure the medicine has worn off. Hold him on the edge and tell him the child is dead before you throw him over. It will give him something to think about on his way down the five-hundred-foot fall. I will have a plan for Casey upon your return." The Queen waved her hand in the direction of the door, motioning for them to go.

As the two of them headed out the door and down the hall, Bolton stopped. "Did you hear something?" He looked down the hall to the opposite end of the Queen's bedroom. It was dimly lit. Casey had closed all the other doors in the hallway to help keep any noise from disturbing the Queen as she was resting.

"Come on, you're hearing things. Thank God the doctor drugged her last night!" Keagan replied.

They continued down the stairs, through the lower court, and came to the servant's pantry. Bolton looked around for something to eat. He spotted some bread and motioned Keagan to sit. Bolton tore the bread in half as they both sat down. "We may not be so lucky next time if we fail her again. Hurry and eat then we will take care of Burgess." Bolton said as he placed his sword on the table.

Meanwhile, back in the hallway, Casey came out from the shadows of an alcove near the Queen's quarters. She heard the whole conversion between the Queen and the two guards. She quietly made her way downstairs. At the bottom of the stairs, she paused to listen for the two guards. Hearing their voices coming from the direction of the pantry, she cut through the king's courtyard which led to the rear entrance of the doctor's office. As she reached the door, she peered through one of the side windows of the entrance. Feeling confident that she wasn't seen, she opened the door to the doctor's quarters slowly and slithered into the room.

The doctor was seated in the darkness with his head in his hands. He had spent the whole night after the delivery worried about his own role in the infant's fate and wishing that there was more, he could do. Where was Poppel? Had he reached Mr. Zs safely? All night long this agony tore at him. Casey put her index finger to her lips and softly "shushed" the doctor as he was starting to stand up with a look of concern on his face. She quietly closed the door behind her.

"We need to get out of here! Keagan and Bolton are on their way to kill us per the Queen's orders!" Casey was noticeably terrified. "Why, why kill us? What is going on Dr. Burgess?" She stood up demanding that he makes some sense of it all.

Dr. Burgess grabbed her by the hand, opened the door, and peeked down the hallway. "Come on; there is no time! We need to get to the stable before they realize we are gone."

Pulling Casey by the hand, Dr. Burgess led her quietly down the hall to the back entrance. Once at the stable, she opened the side door. There was no time for putting saddles on the horses. Casey grabbed bridles for two horses and made her way to the large barn door on the opposite side. She helped the doctor up on his horse, slung the door open, and then jumped on hers. Casey led the way out.

"We must get to Mr. Z to see if Poppel has told him of the child," the doctor explained as they headed for the Roundabout. Casey, who was in front, turned around because she heard the doctor suddenly let out a loud moan. She saw Dr. Burgess crouched over, trying to keep his balance to not fall off his horse. What happened next seemed as if it were a dream… everything unfolded in slow motion, allowing her to watch every little detail… even though it was all in a flash.

First, she noticed the tip of an arrow protruding from the doctor's chest. Looking behind the doctor, she saw Bolton on one knee, reaching behind his back, and drawing another arrow from his quiver. Keagan stood beside him holding the reins of two horses. Then, another arrow pierced the doctor's chest, taking him to the ground. Casey screamed his name, as a numb disbelief overcame her. The doctor lay motionless beside his horse. Bolton was reloading his bow with a third arrow that Casey knew was meant for her. Without a thought, she kicked her horse on both of its sides; it let out a loud neigh and, at once, galloped away toward the Black Forest at top speed. Keagan and Bolton now mounted their horses to give chase. They got to where the doctor was laying. Keagan dismounted to check on him and pronounced, "He's dead."

"Good!… save us the trip to Devil's Cliff and having to throw him off," Bolton replied with a smile.

Keagan spotted Casey disappearing into the forest, "What about her? I am never going in that forest again!"

"Let her go. She'll never find her way through the forest... no threat of her coming back after what she has seen here!"

Then turning to more practical matters concerning his own survival, he said, "We must hide this body from the Queen as it didn't exactly go the way she wanted it to. Let's throw the good doctor in the dung pit. Good place as any to rot," Bolton offered with an obviously unashamed, sarcastic tone. He grabbed the arms and motioned for Keagan to take the doctor's legs. They carried the body around the back of the stable where there was a large pit full of dung, covered over with straw. They positioned themselves on one edge and swung the doctor's body into the pit. They each grabbed a pitchfork and hurriedly shoveled in new straw to cover him up.

"We are not done with Casey! We will hunt her down!" Bolton vowed, "I don't care if it takes the rest of my life to find her. Telling the Queen one lie is bad enough; let's not lie about Casey."

fter what felt like hours of riding, Tippet finally reached Fullerton's home and knocked on the front door. A short, heavy-set boy, around fourteen years of age, opened the door. He had a round face, dark eyes, and pitch-black hair. In one hand he was holding a small loaf of bread.

"Tippet, what are you doing here? And why are you sweating and out of breath?" the young man asked as he put the loaf to his mouth and proceeded to rip a piece off with his teeth.

"I have no time to tell the whole story Nate. Throw on some shoes and a coat, grab a weapon, and get a horse from your barn. Quickly!" Tippet demanded. Nate's face tightened. Handing the bread to Tippet, he turned and bent down beside the doorway to put his shoes on.

"And why do you need a weapon, Tippet?

"We may not. Now, come on! stop the questions and hurry up!" Tippet replied.

"We?" Nate said, heading in the direction of the kitchen.

"Yes, your membership in the Society compels you. Mr. Z needs our help. You know what to do," Tippet gave Nate a knowing look.

Grabbing a knife that was on a cutting board, Nate turned to a panel in the wall. Undoing a small latch, the panel swung open revealing a hidden alcove. He retrieved two black-hooded robes, handing one to Tippet. Then, squeezing past Tippet through the narrow front doorway, Nate hurried off in the direction of the barn. When he next emerged, he was on top of a chestnut-colored mare.

"Here, this is all I could find in the barn for a weapon. I grabbed this serrated knife out of the kitchen," Nate said as he handed Tippet a short double-sided hatchet. "Let me know along the way exactly what the hell I am getting into." The two men pulled the dark hoods over their heads and started for the forest.

Tippet told Nate as much as he was briefed by Mr. Z. Details do not matter when a life is on the line. The terrain was tough on the horse's hooves; the slippery moss and bulging roots from the trees slowed their pace. The air grew colder and damper. The foot of Grim Rock was about two hundred yards ahead of them when Nate suddeningly pointed to the ground ahead of them on their right.

"Look, over there… something on the ground!" He said, dismounting and holding the reins of his horse while walking closer to the object. Tippet also got down and tried to see what Nate was looking at. On the ground, covered in a heavy film of dew, was the basket the child was in. Nate picked it up and looked at Tippet with a worried look.

"Search around for any sign, especially a rock pile of sorts." Tippet ordered, as he too was afraid that they were too late to save the baby. They searched within a hundred-yard- radius, all the way up to where Grim Rock started to shoot up out of the earth. At that point, it became so steep and moss-covered, that no one could scale it.

Suddenly, they found two sets of fresh horse tracks. Overcome by hopelessness, Tippet sighed, "We are too late; the child must have perished."

"He could still be alive, Tippet. We need to keep looking," Nate responded, desperately scanning the darkening surroundings for piles of rocks.

"No Nate; It has been over four hours. We haven't heard a cry of a child. We just have an empty bed. They probably took the child and left it to die on the other side. Who knows? We should go back and tell Mr. Z that there is no hope. The child is dead," Tippet said as he mounted his horse, and turned to head back.

"They will pay for this evil!" Nate swore as he tied the basket to his saddle, got on his horse, and followed Tippet.

Tippet and Nate raced through the forest towards Mr. Z's shop. Just as they were approaching the Roundabout entrance, Tippet saw another rider about fifty yards ahead of them. He could tell that it was a woman from her floating hair and slender figure. He also thought he heard a few sobs coming from her direction. He dug his heels into his horse's side, wanting to catch up with her before reaching the entrance.

"Hello, are you in trouble?" Tippet shouted out as he got closer. He expected some sort of an answer. Instead, however, she dug her heels into her own horse to speed away, seemingly to avoid any contact with Tippet. He easily caught up to her, though, reached out, and grabbed the reins of her horse, yelling, "Whoaaaa". The horse obeyed. They both stopped abruptly.

"What are you doing? I must get to the Roundabout!" she complained as she tried to pull the reins away from Tippet. By now, Nate caught up to them and positioned himself on the other side of the girl. Who were these strange, hooded figures she wondered. She looked at them with their mysterious garb, hoods obscuring their faces, and thought, "Oh no! They are going to do something bad to me! Maybe they work for the Queen." Images of Bolton and Keagan resurfaced as her heart rate soared. Then she looked at Tippet's horse and got down off her own horse.

She grabbed the basket that was tied to his saddle, and with a loud, demanding voice asked, "Where did you get this basket? Who are you two?"

51

Tippet hesitated. He couldn't reveal too much to a stranger, for her own protection as much as theirs. He looked warily at Nate.

"Well, who are you?" he shot back, ignoring her question.

From the moment Casey spotted the basket, her present fears vanished. Her concern shifted back entirely to the safety of the child. "Please, you must tell me where you found this; it's extremely important!"

Tippet was still cautious about informing a stranger about anything. She did seem, on the other hand, to have intimate knowledge of the child and its whereabouts. At that moment, he decided it would be best to let Mr. Z handle this. "I cannot tell you now," he said, "But come with us, if you will, to the home of our friend, and he may have answers for you."

"Who is your friend?" she asked timidly.

"His name is Mr. Zimmerman. Come along."

Hmm… Zimmerman… Could that be the Mr. Z that Dr. Burgess had spoken of? She decided to go along with the two hooded figures despite her consternation. "Alright," she replied as she began to mount her horse. She then yanked the reins from Tippet's grip, who was taken off guard by her strength and forcefulness. Finally, the three of them rode off in silence for Mr. Z's.

The Roundabout was aptly named since it had a common in the center of a circular street lined by shops of all kinds. Casey looked in awe. This was the first time she had been off the Kingdoms' grounds since Queen Mara "rescued" (that's the word used by the Queen) her from her village. Sadly, it was full of revolving men, drunkenness, and sickness. Casey was thankful in the beginning for the Queen's kindness; but, after so many days of being Mara's private chambermaid, Casey learned that first impressions of someone are not always a true picture of their inner personality or character. She often wondered how her life would have played out had she remained in that house. Could one scenario be any better or worse than the other? …either the physical abuse from Bolton and Keagan, or that of strange men in her former life? Was the emotional abuse she suffered from the Queen any worse than the abuse she suffered at the hands of the women who made themselves available for men to endlessly degrade them? She visibly shook her head and dispelled the memories. At least in this very moment, she was free from all her abusers. She felt both giddy and terrified at the same time.

They arrived at a store with a big sign on the front that read "The Toy Box." Mr. Z was a toymaker, furniture-maker, and carpenter. Tippet knocked with a special combination that consisted of two rapid knocks, one slow one with a pause, and followed by two more rapid ones. The door opened slowly. Mr. Z grabbed Tippet by the hand and pulled him in hurriedly, Nate and Casey followed them into the store. Mr. Z then led them to the workshop area in the back of the building. On the far side of the room was a small bed. A girl, who couldn't have been more than one year old, was sleeping peacefully under a blanket. "Please try to keep your voices down so as not to wake up my sweet daughter, Jillian," Mr. Z asked in a low voice.

Tippet, Nate, and Casey sat down on a long bench; Mr. Z remained standing. He scrutinized Casey and said, "I'm Mr. Zimmerman. Most people call me Mr. Z. And who are you, my child?"

Casey let out a gasp of relief as soon as she heard him say "Mr. Z." She thought about how strange this whole day had been; she did manage to find the man she was searching for, but it felt as if some mysterious force was directing her path.

"My name is Casey. Dr. Burgess told me to come to you. He said you would be able to help, and you know other people who can too. But I am not comfortable talking in front of these two strangers," Casey said as she tried to keep her composure, although a tear escaped from her eye.

"I am sorry Miss but right now, you are a stranger to the three of us as well. I can assure you, though, that Tippet and Nate are completely trustworthy. I hold them in the highest regard, knowing them since their childhood. Please, my dear, tell me why Dr. Burgess sent you to me? And how is he doing, by the way?" Mr. Z asked this as he leaned back against the workbench, steadying himself.

Casey looked to the ground and with a soft voice said, "Dr. Burgess is dead! Bolton, Mara's captain of the guard, shot two arrows through his chest while we were trying to escape from Hagen." Casey hesitated as she felt her eyes well up and the knot in her throat release. She began to sob, "I wanted to help him, I did! But If I had tried to help him, I would have suffered the same fate." Casey became hysterical the way one does when they begin to process the reality of a brush with death or just having witnessed a murder. For Casey, it had been both.

Tippet and Nate looked at one another in disbelief of the horrible news. "Why would someone kill the doctor? That man devoted his life tending to the sick. He didn't care who it was and never favored one over another. He just wanted to help others," Nate exclaimed, looking down at the floor, shaking his head. Flashes of his friend, Dr. Burgess, flooded his head. He pictured the good man smiling.

Mr. Z put his hands to his face. The two men knew that he was crying and instantly understood that it was for more than just Dr. Burgess.

Casey got up and put her hand on Mr. Z's shoulder, trying to console him. These three strangers seemed to know Dr. Burgess better than she herself did. Here she was, reaching out to one of them in compassion, and sharing his grief. This all felt like a bad dream. It was so surreal. Nonetheless, it must be remembered that the common thread in all of this remains the welfare of an innocent child.

Mr. Z tapped her hand as he straightened up, and then wiped his eyes. He recalled that he and the doctor never saw eye to eye on so many matters; yet Dr. Burgess was so gracious at the time of Mr. Z's wife's illness. Mr. Z had then seen a kindness in the doctor that he had not expected. Memories suddenly resurfaced of when Dr. Burgess had stayed for a few days by his beloved wife's bedside trying to make her comfortable as she lay dying from pneumonia. He turned back to Casey with a quivering voice and said, "Please Casey, continue. I am sorry; I am truly sorry you had to witness such a horrific thing as that." Mr. Z encouraged her to continue relating her story as he covered her hand with his and nodded solemnly.

"I really don't know where to start, sir. It was Queen Mara; she ordered the guards to kill him, and then they were to kill me next. Thankfully, I was able to overhear the plot while I hid outside her chambers. I hurried to warn the doctor. We made it to the stable and were able to get on horseback. Unfortunately, Bolton and Keagan managed to track us down. Bolton shot and struck the doctor twice through the back, killing him. I saw Bolton reloading a third time, but I was able to escape. So here I am." Casey concluded."

"Why did Mara want you and the doctor dead?" Mr. Z asked.

"I guess it was only because we were there and witnessed everything. It was late last night. The Queen cried out in anguish. I came to her aid. There was blood all over the bedsheets. Dr. Burgess came soon after me. The Queen... she... She gave birth to a boy! No one, except the doctor, knew she was with child. I couldn't believe it. She hid it so well, even from me — her chambermaid. The baby was in distress. The doctor cut her stomach twice to save the child. It was horrible! I had to hold the Queen down and she fainted. When she recovered, she had an alarming and puzzling disdain for the newborn. How could a mother hate her own child? What sort of a person is she? The Queen cringed when she saw him for the first time and waved him away..." Casey then continued babbling, with gut-wrenching memories of the past twenty-four hours gushing out of her.

"Wait," Casey suddenly realized, "you should have already known about all of this. Dr. Burgess said he sent Poppel here to tell you. Did he make it?"

"Yes, Poppel got here, but with just the news of the child and its impending fate… nothing else… nothing about the doctor and you. As soon as I could, I sent Tippet and Nate here to confront Bolton and Keagan. Don't be fooled by their age for they are very competent and trustworthy with such matters," Mr. Z said as he looked at the two of them, anticipating their report.

Tippet stood up. He put his hand on Casey's shoulder and said, "I'm sorry about the doctor, and I'm glad you were able to escape." As he reached down to his side to lift the basket, he explained in a somber voice to Mr. Z, "This is all we found at the foot of Grim Rock. We searched a hundred yards out from where it was. Nothing, and no sign of Bolton and Keagan… or the child. I'm sorry, we must have been too late to save the baby. They must have taken him deeper into the woods. Because of the terrain, we could not track them any further. There was not a single clue left there by the two guards, save this empty basket." Tippet bemoaned all of this with a defeated look on his face.

Mr. Z stood up straight, looking at the three of them, and said, "I know you all tried your best and should know that in your hearts. The child is in a better place. As for Bolton and Keagan, their fate will be dramatically different. Ahead of them waits a place of eternal unrest, a volcano of bitterness that erupts from one's soul for all eternity. Penalties of such evil are punishable not only in the body, but also in the mind and soul. They shall cry in damnation, but their cries will never be heard — even by those that are there with them. Indeed, they shall even scream out, but will never be heard." Mr. Z paused as he found himself becoming enraged at the thought of these human beings having a total disregard for life. He refocused and turned his attention back to the three young adults and thought about how they must be feeling inside now.

"So, remember, especially now, that when you are hurting inside, this life goes by in the blink of an eye, whereas the next life is eternal.

However, there, in that place, your intentions will be revisited and then judged accordingly. These are the deeds of an evil woman who seeks to blind others from the truth using her lies." Mr. Z then stood over his daughter who was nestled under the covers, fast asleep.

The three of them gazed at him, waiting for him to continue, for they never heard anyone talk to them like that. He had a quiet confidence in his words that was captivating and each meaning he purveyed strengthened his pillar-like voice and gave all who were present a sense of hope.

After Mr. Z finished preaching, Tippet approached him and whispered, "How do you know this girl is telling the truth? We don't know her. She is from Hagen."

"Look at her; she is just a child. Why would she risk coming here, through the forest, to the opposite kingdom? It is obvious that she is in danger. Also, her story lines up with what Poppel told me, and she knows of the basket and other details," Mr. Z calmly reasoned. "Until I have evidence she is lying, I will take her at her word; and so, should you, Tippet. Now, go to Nate's. All of you need a good meal and a good night's rest. Come back in the morning, all three of you." Mr. Z said.

The three of them did exactly as Mr. Z asked. Making their way through the cold of the evening, not uttering a single word all the way to Nate's, they each pondered in their minds the seriousness of the day's events.

After this meeting, nothing more was heard of the child. Mr. Z made inquiries where he could, but they came to nothing. Casey, for her part, never gave up hope, knowing there was nothing she could do. She settled down in the Roundabout and worked as Mr. Z's housekeeper, eventually becoming more like a daughter to him.

eanwhile, days went by like minutes. Sandra and Ben raised Jack as their own son, as Darcia watched undetected in their shadows. They kept Jack in the village, isolated from the outside world. There were many other children who lived there but there was no formal schooling for them. The village, albeit poor, had many brilliant people living in it from all walks of life. These were silver linings from the fallout of the Great War. For all the death, destruction, and pain it left behind, there were benefits as well. The world instantly became smaller, not in the size of land, but in population. It was a new beginning, the optimistic believed. A greater sense of belonging and community now existed. People were once again dependent on a neighbor rather than a form of government. This is what led to the villages being established. They became self-sufficient. They were dotted around the outskirts of Black Forest. Clearwater was the one at the source of the Crystal River. This is where Jack spent the first six years of his life.

Jack's mind was like a sponge; he soaked everything up. Sandra and Ben were exhausted some days, hoping he would eventually stop asking so many questions and just play with his toys like the rest of the boys in the village. He was very smart and learned from anyone who was willing to take the time to teach him. Along with his inquisitive mind, he also was very imaginative. He would look at things from different angles, turning them inside out, right side up, and upside down, to see if he could change them or solve a problem.

Jack was also handsome and pleasant to look at. He had warm hazel eyes, light brown hair, and a sturdy build. Sandra and Ben, for lack of knowing otherwise, made Jack's birth date the same as the day he came to live with them, the first day of April. They somehow knew that it was important to keep that original day, regardless of how things transpired nearly six years ago. A person's birthday is a day of celebration of one's life, and for Jack it was the foundation of his roots. As each day passed, it got easier to believe that Jack was their child, and slowly they lost all stress from the need to hide Jack's identity.

As Jack grew older, he began to question why they never went to the Roundabout to trade, shop, and socialize like the other families from the village did. At first, he thought it was a game, and that someday it would be his turn to go; but over time, it became increasingly obvious to him that he was the only one not allowed to leave the village. Day after day he would hound his parents to take him to the shops, especially Mr. Z's Toy Box (He would often hear the other children rant and rave about it, as they would show him their new toys that their parents bought them). Of course, every request by Jack to go there was denied using one excuse after another. Jack's frustration mounted. He was, nevertheless, extremely strong-willed, and filled with curiosity. "Why is it that I am the only one who can't leave the village?" he would ask himself. "What is wrong with me that I can't go? What are my parents hiding from me, and why?"

One night after his parents tucked him in for bed, he got up and felt around under his mattress, pulled out a canvas bag, and started filling it with a change of clothes. He sat on the end of his bed waiting patiently for his parents to go to sleep. He then cracked his bedroom door open, checked on his parents' bedroom door, saw that it was closed tight, and tiptoed to the kitchen. There he grabbed some bread and fruit, stuffed them in his bag, and headed for the front door. He stopped to put on his shoes, turned the knob, looked back towards his parents' bedroom once more, and then slid out the door.

Until now, Jack had only been down the main road as far as the vegetable farm. From that point on, he was clueless about which way to go. Not having any sense of how far it was from the village to the Roundabout, he began his journey by faith, one would say — blind faith. The moon was full, lighting his path. He didn't plan on it but considered it a good omen that tonight was the right night to leave.

After an hour of walking, Jack began to get somewhat spooked by all the eerie sounds along the way. Nighttime is very different when out walking in it than simply hearing it outside one's own secure bedroom window while lying in a comfortable bed. Those noises were all around him now and they felt too close for comfort. With each step in the direction of the Roundabout, he felt more alone and insecure in his decision. Self-doubt was beginning to grab a hold of him. He stopped on the side of the road, sat on a boulder, and pulled out some bread from his sack, hoping it would distract him from all the various ominous noises surrounding him. As he chewed the fresh bread, his mind went back and forth, debating the pros and cons of his current state. For the first time, he questioned whether in fact this was a wise thing to do. Perhaps if he just would have waited a little longer, his parents would have taken him to the Roundabout. On the other hand, he felt that it was a great adventure. Parents would only take all the fun out of it, he reasoned. They were always overly cautious and strict. Ahead of him, just up the road, stood a great mystery of unseen shops, a whole new world. Behind him remained the familiar, the predictable, the mundane.

Of course, the "pros" had won, given Jack's utterly curious nature. A smile came to Jack's face as he stood up. He stuffed the bread back into his sack, brushed his bottom off, and threw the sack back over his shoulder. Once again, he continued down the road towards his adventure. He did not know at all what lay ahead. Adventures do not always play out the way you would imagine. With miles of excitement to go (yet with traces of lingering fear), he now felt repurposed, confident enough in his decision to go on.

He walked on for hours, anticipating all the things in the Roundabout that he had heard so much about from the neighborhood kids. The sun was just starting to peek on the horizon behind him. Birds began singing to the new day on the rise. There were all sorts of four-legged creatures scurrying across the road ahead of him. Daylight brought a stronger sense of security. "What a perfect day for an adventure," he thought.

To his delight, he saw a wide opening ahead. As he drew closer, his feet felt lighter causing his pace to increase as he seemed to shift into another gear. With a hop and a skip, there it stood, all shining from the sun's reflection: the Roundabout! Jack finally got that coveted glimpse of the circular road surrounding the large town-commons. There were paths leading through the commons from all four sides, all meeting in the center. "I am a kid living in a dream," he thought to himself. There was not a soul in sight currently. He picked the closest pathway and headed into the commons. It was bigger than he had imagined.

The center was lined with benches that surrounded a small fish-pond. Jack soaked it all in. He would have enjoyed sitting and resting a bit had it not been his first time there. There were ducks in the pond and trees planted along the cobblestone paths. He found himself walking faster, anticipating what there was to see next. In the distance he noticed some buildings with different shops in them. They were much bigger than any of the ones in his village. As Jack drew closer, he saw a storefront that had large windows and a double door in the front. The sign over the door read, "Pete's Tavern." He had heard stories of this pub from some of the men in the village about how people would drink from dawn to midnight, singing and telling jokes. Occasionally, fistfights would break out there, sometimes so big that they would spill out onto the street. As he stood there, he let out a chuckle thinking that it was quiet now. "Maybe they ran out of moonshine," he half-jokingly said to himself. He shrugged his shoulders and continued on his way.

Next, he turned down Pennington Lane, the main street that circled the Roundabout. He noticed a smaller store next to the tavern that had one large window and a single door. Its sign read "Finch's." "Hmmm," Jack wondered, "What could that be?" Looking closer through the window, he saw a man, fully dressed in a three-piece costume. He was very slender and motionless. Jack banged on the glass, yelling "hello", but there was no reply from the frozen man; he didn't even move an inch. "That's odd!" he thought.

He pressed on to the next storefront. Looking up above the front door, he noted a blue, red, and yellow sign saying, "The Toy Box". The front of the store had two large windows which wrapped in the center to create a recess where the door was located. This configuration was designed for the sole purpose of grabbing the shoppers' eyes, pulling them along the full display of toys, right to the entrance door. Jack took a good while to get to that door; he was too intrigued by the many different toys that were on display just on the single large bottom shelf. "How lucky," he thought, "to be a kid growing up in the Roundabout… to be able to come here every day!"

Looking through the glass window, he saw lots of dolls wearing various styles of elegant dresses. He also saw a horse-drawn carriage with two hand-carved and painted horses harnessed to it. Separate pieces surrounded them: farmers, millers and craftsmen stood all around the center piece, that of a perfect replica of the Roundabout.

Jack put his hands on the glass, amazed at how everything looked so real. He was half-expecting the horses to start pulling the carriage, and the wooden figurines to start moving. He remained there, in awe, for what seemed to be hours.

Suddenly he heard a voice say, "Little boy, what are you doing out here so early and alone?"

Jack turned with surprise to see the source of the voice. Directly across the street and coming towards him, was a tall, thin girl with strawberry blonde hair. Jack stood motionless as she came right up to him.

"Didn't you hear me? I don't remember ever seeing you around here before," the girl wanted to know as she looked into Jack's eyes. She turned her head slightly back and forth to scan his face. She had seen him before; but, when and where? It did not come to her right away as she looked at the boy a little closer.

"My name is Jack. I was just looking at all the toys," he said as he pointed to the storefront window. "Who are you? Have you seen these toys? When will the shopkeeper open the store?" Jack quizzed the girl, hoping she was the owner or at least had a key.

"My name is Casey. Yes, I have indeed seen them before. I've painted most of them." Casey proudly replied as she continued to search her memory for where she may have seen this boy before. Up close, she now could see that he was so familiar to her.

"This is my very first time here." Jack said. "Where do you live, Jack?" Casey asked.

"In the villages," Jack was starting to get this sinking feeling that he was in trouble. "And your mom and dad, do they know where you are?" Casey was trying not to make Jack nervous. She was afraid he would stop answering her questions, so she had to think them through carefully.

"Well, no; I sort of came here on my own. Are you going to tell on me, Miss?" Jack was hoping she wouldn't. Oh, the trouble he would be in.

"My name is Casey. Don't you think they'll be worried to see that you aren't in your bed when they wake up?" Casey was walking on thin ice, and she knew it. She was playing the guilt card and hoping it would cause Jack to realize how they may be feeling right about now.

"Well, I snuck out of the house after I was sure they were asleep," Jack responded as he looked to the ground.

"I will make a deal with you," Casey offered as she reached into her other pocket and pulled out a silver key ring and shook a set of keys in front of his eye's. "Guess what these keys open?" Casey saw Jack pointing to the front door of the Toy Box. "Yep, that door right behind you!" Casey proclaimed as she began to walk towards the door. Reaching it, she unlocked it. She then turned to Jack to motion him in. Jack almost tripped as both of his legs began to walk at the same time. He was so excited.

"I will let you look around at all the toys; you can pick one, only one." Casey proposed, knowing that the boy would do anything just to have one. "But first, you must promise that you will let me take you home.

Jack shook his head up and down, and let out a quick "yes," as he surveyed the shelves wondering what to look at first. He wanted one of everything.

"Alright, pick one toy. Then we will clean you up and have some breakfast before we hit the road, Jack," Casey said as she put her hand on Jack's shoulder and guided him into the store.

Jack felt overwhelmed; there was so much to see. "This could take all day," he thought. He first went over to the window display of the Roundabout scene. Next, he turned to see dolls, the size of real babies, sitting in painted wooden wagons. Some were too big to carry on such a long journey home, he concluded. Then he stopped in his tracks as he reached for a figurine. It was vibrant with color: red, blue, yellow, and white. It had a big smile, rosy cheeks, and a costume covering it from head to toe. This figurine had hair that seemed to be growing out of it, like a burning bush aglow.

Casey was honored by his choice and so she began to say, "Jack, you have picked one of my favorites, the one I am most proud of, and a favorite of many, young and old. I call him "Chester". His costume is his disguise. He is a trickster, a performer, and, most importantly, he will make you laugh. All you need is an imagination and "Chester" can be and do anything you wish. Now come with me out in the back. I will get us something to eat, and you can clean up. Then we can start the return trip home." Casey said as she guided Jack through the doorway into the back room, closing it behind her.

As Jack sat eating his breakfast, fork in one hand, "Chester" in the other, Casey was staring at him. She was trying to come up with a list of questions to ask Jack's parents for when they would reach his home.

"Alright Jack, are you ready to hit the road?" Casey asked. Jack nodded his head, yes. Then let's head next door to see if Mr. Fletcher's stables are open." Casey said, motioning Jack to come with her.

Jack reached for and opened his sack of clothing. He then wrapped "Chester" carefully in a shirt that he pulled out of it. Finally, he placed the enveloped doll back in the sack, closed it again and threw it over his shoulder. "Yes, Miss Casey," he respectfully replied.

When they walked into the stables, they saw Mr. Fletcher throwing an armful of hay over a stall door. He was a good-natured man, short, stumpy looking, with a full beard and dark eyes. "Miss Casey, you are up early. Who is that fine-looking young man accompanying you?" Mr. Fletcher playfully asked as he wiped his forehead with a handkerchief.

"Good morning, Sir. This is Jack. He has taken it upon himself to go on an adventure unbeknownst to his parents back in Clearwater.

We made a pact. He was able to choose from any toy in the shop and, in exchange, I would take him back home to his parents. I explained that they would be delirious with worry, upon finding him missing." Casey said as she saddled her horse with no objection from Mr. Fletcher.

"Nice to meet you, Jack. And what toy did you pick? I know you had lots to choose from and so it couldn't have been easy." Mr. Fletcher said as he helped Casey with the saddle straps.

"I picked Chester," Jack declared with a smile from ear to ear as he raised the toy out of his sack to show it off.

Mr. Fletcher turned to Casey with a surprised look and said, "Jack, Chester is very special. You are a lucky boy!" He turned back to Casey and gave her a wink of approval. "How 'bout I pick out a horse for the young man?"

"Yes please. A pony with a quiet and patient spirit if you have one to rent for the day," Casey answered.

"Of course," Mr. Fletcher responded. "Daisy would fit that description to a tee. She may not be the fastest in the lot, but she is the smartest. She will get you there and back blindfolded, although you may be last to the dinner table." Mr. Fletcher saddled Daisy, then lifted Jack up on top of the pony, handed him the reins, and gave him a smile.

Casey and Jack waved goodbye, thanking Mr. Fletcher as they headed down Pennington Lane. Jack had a modest grin on his face for he felt confident with Casey by his side to escort him home. He was hopeful his parents would not be so angry at him for leaving in the middle of the night. Thus far, his adventure could not have gone any better. Casey's mind wasn't as sure as Jack's was when it came to meeting his parents. She was expecting them to be quite unhappy with Jack. She knew Sandra, having met her in the Roundabout upon occasion. Casey recalled that Sandra always kept to herself, and so her greetings were always quick, vague, and emotionless. Casey was hoping that Sandra's husband would be a more engaging conversationalist.

ack at the Roundabout, Mr. Fletcher finished feeding the horses and went inside to have his second cup of coffee when he heard a rider approaching. Walking out with coffee in hand, he saw one of Hagen's guards heading slowly towards his stable side door. He sipped some coffee as he waited for the guard to get closer. He recognized him as soon as he was near enough to make out his face. It was Bolton. Bolton stopped about six feet in front of Mr. Fletcher.

"Morning Fletcher, you're up early as usual I see. Seen anyone out of the ordinary this week?" Bolton asked, disguising his tone to seem friendly.

"No Bolton, not today," Fletcher replied as he looked downward to his feet. "Same as every week you ask me."

Bolton was pretty good at sensing when someone was hiding something from him, and he was getting a strong notion of this from Fletcher. He dismounted, stood in Fletcher's face, put his right hand on his sword, and replied, "I asked about this week, not *today*," Bolton shouted out as he took a step back, looking at the large stable.

Then he went in the side door, looked in the stalls, and quickly turned back around in the direction of Mr. Fletcher. "Your stable looks somewhat depleted. Rent some out this morning, did you? How many?

One? Two? More?" Bolton persisted quite forcefully in his line of questioning, knowing that Mr. Fletcher was lying to him. As he walked back out to where Fletcher was standing, he noticed two sets of fresh tracks leading out of the stable.

"No… a few days ago, just some locals rented for a couple of days, wanting to ride a bunch of trails." Fletcher nervously replied, wondering how weak his lie sounded.

Suddenly in one motion, Bolton grabbed Fletcher by the neck and, with his other hand, picked up a pitchfork leaning against a wall. He lifted Fletcher a few inches off the ground and said, "I know now you are lying to me. If you don't start telling me the truth. I am going to fasten you to the wall with this farming tool and watch you bleed out until you die," Bolton threatened through his clenched teeth.

"Did you forget where you are, Bolton? You know what will happen to you. This is the Neutral Zone, not Hagen. You have no authority here and so if you pierce me with that, you will be tried and convicted." Fletcher replied.

"I don't need to remind you of the reason for my line of questioning. For six long years I have been asking you the same questions. I have been coming here every week, taking note of the number of animals in your stable, and one, the chestnut mare kept in that stall that is now empty." As he pointed to it, he added, "We all know that mare belongs to Miss Casey, as you call her. Now tell me the truth or I am going to put an end to you. I *know* you are lying, and I'm not leaving until you tell me where she went and with whom," Bolton declared. He released his grip. Fletcher sank to his knees. With both hands on the farming tool, Bolton pressed it against Fletcher's belly. Fletcher felt the ends pierce his body. Sharp pain shot across his whole stomach.

Fletcher denied any knowledge of Casey or anyone else as he began to feel weakened from loss of blood. His knees buckled. He immediately hunched over, thus causing the long metal ends of the pitchfork to go in deeper without any added effort from Bolton.

Realizing this was the last opportunity to get any information from his victim, Bolton continued his interrogation, "Last chance Fletcher, to save yourself!"

Wanting only to survive and end the pain, Fletcher begged, "Wait! stop! I'll tell you!"

"This better not be another lie. If it is, I will come back and flatten you like horseshoes on an anvil," Bolton warned. He removed the pitchfork from Fletcher's belly and his victim fell to the ground on his back, weakly holding his bleeding gut.

"Miss Casey was here with a little boy; one I've never seen before. He ran away from home to come see the Roundabout. They headed north towards the villages," Fletcher gasped, feeling extremely light-headed and out of breath. "Now that wasn't so difficult." Bolton lifted the pitchfork up again and, this time, plunged the farming tool's pointed tines right through Fletcher's stomach. Bolton watched as Fletcher's eyes slowly closed and he became motionless.

Leaving the pitchfork standing straight up in Fletcher's body, Bolton rinsed his bloody hands in a water trough. He jumped on his horse, and calmly trotted away, taking a path through the woods behind the stables. When he seemed far enough away from the Roundabout, he veered off the path and onto Pennington Lane, galloping quickly towards the Village of Clearwater.

asey and Jack rode down the pot-holed filled road when suddenly, Jack heard Casey give out a loud moan. He at once turned to see her slumped over her horse, with the point of an arrow protruding from her chest. Jack pulled the reins of Daisy back and the horse came to a halt. He dismounted in one motion, ran to her side, and steadied her mare.

"Jack, go! Leave me here!" She said, as she tilted her head towards him to see his face. Jack then looked back down the road in the direction from which the arrow came. In the distance, he saw the figure of a man on one knee. Casey again pleaded for Jack to get on his horse and go, but all his attention was focused on the man who was, by now, standing up. Jack could see him reaching behind his back; he figured it was for another arrow. He looked down the road and felt a panic come over him. Casey was now launched forward all the way onto the horse's neck, almost motionless. There was a fork in the road, not too far ahead. Jack grabbed the reins of Casey's horse and after tying them to his saddle, began heading in that direction. He then heard a whistling sound followed by a thump. At the same time, Casey's horse let out a long high-pitched neigh. Jack looked behind him and, at the same time, felt a pulling on his saddle. Casey's horse took the second arrow high in its rear quarter and thus her brave steed was now in noticeable pain. Jack turned to see that the man was still the same distance away. He concluded that he was a soldier of sorts, one trained in warfare. This man's accuracy at such a great distance was not by chance.

He untied the reins from his saddle and was about to check on Casey when he heard another swoosh in the air. It was another arrow which cut through the wind and landed inches from the first one. This time it went straight through Casey's ribs causing both her and the horse to fall together to the hard ground. They landed with one hard *thud*. Jack jumped down. He got a fix on the assailant and saw that he was now standing and about to jump on his horse. Casey let out a loud moan as a very heavy Daisy was lying on top of her legs, dead.

"Jack," she whispered as she gasped for air. "Jaaaaaaack, goooooo!" She closed her eyes as blood trickled down her chin and onto the hard trail. Jack began to cry. He was in shock. Despite everything, he jumped up on his horse, yelled, and dug his heels into its sides.

The horse responded eagerly, much to Jack's relief. Now approaching the fork in the road around the bend, he sped up as fast as he could, periodically checking behind him to see where the man was. After reaching the bend, he looked back once more and saw that the rider was out of sight. Not being sure which road led back to his village due to all the moment's confusion and uncertainty, he opted to go left.

Meanwhile, the rider stopped where Casey and her horse lay in the middle of the road. Confident he knew where Jack was headed, Bolton stopped and got down from his horse. He drew his bow, loaded it with yet another arrow, and approached the seemingly dead girl. The memory of Casey kicking him in the groin that summer morning and escaping his clutches surfaced in his head. Now was his time to exact revenge. He put his foot on the arrow protruding from her chest and stepped on it with all his weight, waiting to see if she would react. He was half-hoping she would so that he might flaunt his power over her in her last moments on earth, ready to use that third arrow. Convinced she was dead, however, he then rummaged through her clothing, looking for anything that may have to do with Jack: a paper with directions, the name of a village… something that would verify whether it in fact was Jack who was with her. Finding nothing, he headed off in pursuit of the boy in question.

Jack, by this time, began to see some familiar landmarks. He especially knew that he was getting closer to home when he passed by the vegetable gardens. Some of the villagers who were working in the gardens saw Jack on a pony coming down the road. Jack noticed them turning to one another, whispering, and pointing at him. He figured that this was a sign that he was in trouble. It surely seemed as if word had spread quickly of his adventure to the Roundabout. Directly ahead of him stood a group of people in the middle of the road. Out of that crowd, his parents emerged, heading right for him as he got closer.

"Oh, thank God, you're alive!" his mother cried out in relief as she touched his leg, motioning for him to come down into her arms.

Ben was right behind her, with both hands on her shoulders. His facial expression didn't match his wife's initial response upon seeing Jack's safe arrival. He was, after all, the father, and needed to impose his authority; he must enforce the rules! Jack was out of breath and still in shock from experiencing today's horrific event. Sandra sat him down on a boulder by the side of the road and knelt in front of him. She could feel him shaking, his skin clammy from a cold sweat.

"Are you alright? Are you hurt? Where did you go Jack? Where did you get that horse?" Sandra asked as delicately as she could, given the circumstances. Jack broke down in tears.

"I'm so sorry Mom, I snuck out last night. I wanted to go to the Roundabout. It was just supposed to be a quick trip and I meant to be home before you and Dad would wake up. I got there and looked at all the shops; and then I met a girl, Miss Casey. She worked at the Toy Box. She asked me who I was, where I lived, and I told her. She let me pick out this toy, 'Chester'. I named him. He took it out of his satchel to show her and then continued with his story. "Then she made me breakfast. After that, we just went next door to the stable where she rented a horse for me, and we headed home." Jack paused. He hugged his mother tightly and wept again, this time like a baby. Sandra gave a look of concern towards her husband.

"Then there was a man who came up behind us, I don't know who he was. He shot two arrows into Miss Casey's chest; she slumped over her horse and told me to go. I couldn't save her; I tried. I'm so sorry Mommy, she is dead because of me." Jack buried his face in his mother's bosom. She held him tightly, saying, "No Jack, it wasn't your fault; that's not true. Look at me."

Jack stood up straight and looked into his mother's eyes as she held both his hands. Sandra, taking Jack by the hand, began walking towards the house, Ben came along the other side and tenderly kissed Jack on the top of his head. He grabbed hold of Jack's other hand, looked down at him and smiled without saying a word. He knew that it was just not the right time for discipline. He felt that Jack, being a scant six years old, went through more trauma in one day than most people do in a lifetime. Jack still clutched "Chester" tightly in his hand. When they reached the house, Sandra took some water and put it over the fire. Then she took Jack to his bed, sat him down, and told him she was starting a bath for him. She got some fresh clothes, a towel, and a bar of ash soap. She then put them on a table near the tub bucket located in the far corner of the house, separated by a wall with a curtain across the front. After pouring the hot water, she carefully added in just enough cold water to make it perfect for her little boy…

Sandra called, "Jack, come. Your bath is ready. You wash up and I will fix you something to eat. Jack made his way to the bath, stripped down, and got in. He sat there staring into the water, revisiting, in his young mind, the events of the day. Sandra went to the kitchen where Ben was sitting at the table. She sat next to him and asked,

"What do you suppose Jack said to that girl? She may have told others about him… where we live, how he is not allowed out of the village. People will grow suspicious of him, of us!" Sandra put her hand on Ben's.

Ben, having the same concerns as his wife, began to reason, "I don't think it is safe to stay here. We need to pack up and move to another village. What about your sister's? We can say she is ill… needs help, and so we will be gone for a while. In the meantime, once it gets dark, I will take the back trail and look for this girl Casey, to see if what Jack told us is true. I will be careful not to be seen.".

"No!… put my sister in danger too? I just can't do that to her. We need to find a place where no one will know us… make up some story… our house burnt, an illness, something believable." Sandra was starting to cry, quietly though, so Jack wouldn't hear it.

"Let's get a good night's rest tonight, sleep on it. This day has been hard on all of us," Ben said as he stood up and went to check on Jack. As he looked across the room, he saw that Jack was dressed and heading for the kitchen where he sat at the table. Sandra went in and put a plate of fresh fruit and vegetables down in front of him as she placed her other hand on his shoulder. She was thinking of how horrific it must have been for him to watch the girl die a violent death. Jack showed no emotion as he ate the food, seemingly still in shock. Jack then arose and headed for his bed. He opened his sack where "Chester" was hiding, pulled him back out, climbed under the covers, and looked at Chester's smiling, clownish face. He was a reminder for Jack of his friend Casey, and her brief appearance in his life. Exhausted physically and emotionally, he fell fast asleep. Sandra and Ben came to his bedside, each taking a turn kissing him "goodnight" on his forehead.

While all of this was going on, Bolton reached the outskirts of Clearwater. He then slowed his pace down so that he could search for the horse that the boy was riding. He knew that Mr. Fletcher always branded his animals just in case a renter turned out to be a horse thief. Here, Bolton would search everywhere for any horse with the 'High Top Stables' logo, made up of the two letters "H.T." within a circle, branded into its rear hind portion. He got off his horse and started walking down the street to get a better look. Most of the homes in the village had neither a stable, nor even a more modest lean-to attached to the side of the house to shelter any horse. The truth be told, many of these villagers couldn't even afford a horse. This made Bolton's search a lot easier. He reached the last house on the left-hand side of the street where he noticed a chestnut-colored pony tied to a post at the back of the house. He could hear the river close by. He tied his horse to a tree out front and reached inside of a saddle bag. He pulled out two extra reins and then he walked into the backyard to scan the horse. Sure enough, and as clear as day, was the sought-after "H.T." branded into the hindquarters of this horse. He hastily made his way to the front door and knocked on it lightly.

Ben opened the door, looked at Bolton, and asked, "May I help you sir?"

Bolton looked behind Ben, trying to see as much of the inside of the house as he could. He gave Ben a once-over, measuring him up, planning how he would overtake him, and answered, "I hope so. I am looking for a lost child; he is around six years old. He wandered off yesterday from the Kingdom of Hagen. Maybe you may have seen him passing through?" Bolton asked, trying to conceal his lying tone.

"I am so sorry sir. I have not seen him. I do hope he is alright." Ben returned, also trying to lie with as few words as possible.

"Is that your horse around back sir?" Bolton continued with his inquiry. Ben spun his head towards the back of the house, then turned around again to face Bolton, replying, "Well, yes, and no. I rented it from High Top Stables in the Roundabout. I was going to use it to pull a few stumps in the field… trying to expand the garden this season, you know."

"Was that this morning, by any chance, that you rented it?" Bolton pressed Ben further, trying to catch him in another lie. Bolton briefly looked in the direction of where the horse was and said, "It appears to me Mr. Fletcher might not have understood your need; that horse couldn't pull a tooth, let alone a stump," Bolton offered with a smirk.

"Well, that could have been my fault; I was probably too vague describing my need…" Ben said as he felt the tension between them growing by the second. All along, he was wondering if he should slam the door, grab Sandra and Jack, and escape through the back of the house.

"I ask because I just left Mr. Fletcher, you know, the owner of the stables. He said that a young woman and a boy rented a horse this morning too. Did you happen to see them when you were there?" Bolton had one of the extra reins in his hands, poised to take Ben by surprise and strangle him with it. "You know sir…… I…… can't say I did." Ben blurted out as he went to slam the door on Bolton.

By now Sandra was awake and calling out Ben's name. Ben shouted back to her, "Sandra, take Jack and hurry; go out the back now!"

Bolton lunged at Ben from behind with his arms out and holding the reins tightly with both hands. Ben could feel the leather tightening around his throat and so he tried to slip his fingers between them and his neck. Bolton pulled him backwards lifting him off the floor. He tightened his grip with all his might and thus choked Ben so hard that his own fingers began to bleed. Tighter and tighter, Bolton pulled on the reins as Ben's resistance diminished quickly. At the same time, Sandra and Jack were able to slip out the back door. When she reached the bottom of the stairs, she saw two figures, one wearing a black hooded coat, and the other, a white one. The person in white was on a horse holding the reins of another horse. The one dressed in black reached out, picked Jack up, and put him on the vacant horse. Turning to Sandra, he said, "Don't worry. We are friends. We have been told to watch over the boy. I don't have much time to explain. You must trust us! That guard was sent by Mara to kill the boy and anyone else who helps him," the man explained as he tried to conceal his identity. Sandra got a quick glimpse and immediately recognized the man. "Is that you Mr.......? Suddenly, without warning, Sandra let out a loud moan. She grabbed her chest and, looking down, saw the end of an arrow protruding out of her red-stained nightgown. At once, she fell to both knees. She then turned to the black hooded man and whispered in his ear so that Jack could not hear what she said. "Please, take my boy Mr. Z." Looking up at Jack, she screamed for him to go with the two robed people. Sandra then fell face down, lifelessly.

The two figures turned their horses around and began their escape. Another arrow landed in a tree trunk directly in front of Mr. Z. By now, many of the villagers were awake and came to the aid of their neighbors. Some of them were armed with knives and swords, and a few showed up with their bows and arrows, used primarily for hunting. Bolton, at this point, was still at the back of the house. He now had only a few arrows left in his quiver and found himself surrounded. Outnumbered and outmatched, he did not dare reach for another arrow to reload. He realized it was a fight or flee situation, so he decided to exercise his third option. He would try and reason with the armed and angry mob. All the villagers were aware of the Neutral Zone's laws governing all lands outside of each Kingdom's boundaries, and the delicate peace those laws were meant to protect. They all saw Sandra lying dead in a pool of blood, and, although not visible to them, deduced that Ben and Jack must have been in the house, presumably dead also. They closed in on Bolton to within ten feet.

Bolton decided to say nothing at all as he made his way back to his horse, the villagers now forming a semi-circle around him. One of the villagers yelled out, "Kill him!" while others reasoned aloud, "No, he must be tried before the Great Council". Bolton packed his quiver and bow onto his saddle as he watched for the villagers' next move against him. Another villager shouted, "Let him go; he will be found out and judged." Bolton, now more confident of being able to ride out of the village unharmed, turned his horse back towards the way he came. He gave one last look to the rear of the house from where the two hooded people snatched Jack and fled. As he began to leave, a few of the villagers having gone inside the house, called out to the rest of them, "Ben was murdered too!" Upon hearing this, Bolton wisely kicked his horse and galloped out of town, never to look back, as he disappeared out of their sight.

In the meantime, the two riders carrying their precious cargo made their way into the Black Forest. Understandably so, Jack was once again in a state of shock which compelled him to have an extra-tight grip around his white-hooded ally. The trail was narrow and overgrown with brush and branches. Deeper in, they pushed on. Mr. Z pointed to his left. They slowed their pace and went off-trail. Jack sensed that this was somehow planned. They reached a large hedgerow and there, riding behind it to one side, was a beautiful, gilded carriage, in red with royal drapery, and carrying ensigns of the Kingdom of Windermere. Jack was amazed; "how did this get here? It must have dropped out of the sky!" Jack marveled as his two personal escorts placed him in the carriage. They then began hooking up the yolk and harness to the two horses. Jack heard someone else approaching. He peered through the narrow opening between the curtains on the carriage door and saw a horse with a stubby, rounded figure-of-a-man emerge from the thicket. The other two riders didn't seem concerned one bit about this new stranger.

"I got here as fast as I could. I didn't want Bolton to see me leaving the village. It appeared he was heading back through town," the rider offered as he got off his horse and tied his reins to a tree. The three of them finally hitched two of the horses to the wagon and tied the other in the back. On foot, they slowly led the carriage out to the main road, all three of them carefully covering their path and footprints with branches and leaves. The two hooded people joined Jack in the coach. The other man climbed up onto the rider's bench, grabbed the reins, and started to drive the coach down the road. Inside, Jack was in awe of the carriage's design, beauty, and comfort. It was for royalty or someone rich, he thought. Like magic, it calmed him in some way, distracting him from all the previous, horrendous calamities he faced. The seats were covered in plush material, colored in deep reds and black. Even the roof inside was upholstered; it was draped in a lighter red fabric with gold-colored tassels.

Jack looked at the black-robed person and asked, "Who are you and why does the Queen want to kill me and who told you to watch over me? I'm just a boy. My parents are poor. What business of the Queen, am I?" Jack then turned to the white-robed person, expecting one of them to answer his questions. "Jack, it is best we don't tell you anymore than you already know. It is too dangerous. In time, you will know everything. For now, you must trust us to make decisions for you. We are now on our way to find you a safe place to live. No one there will know who you are or what has happened. We will be watching just as we have been, and we will protect you from the Queen and others," the person in the white hood explained.

"Protect me? My parents are dead; Miss Casey is dead. Who knows who will be next... maybe you two! And you are not very good at disguising your voice, Miss. What shall I call you?" Jack brashly asked her.

"Hush! You needn't call me anything. Come now, we have a long journey ahead of us. I think it best if you lay there on the other seat. Under it, you will find a blanket. We will talk more when you are awake." She put her hand on his shoulder, helped him to the other bench, and grabbed a blanket to cover him up. Finally, she kissed him on his forehead. A tear began to flow from one of her eyes as she sat back next to the man. The road was filled with potholes. The man reached for a smaller blanket under his seat and placed it under Jack's head. He too kissed Jack on the forehead yet did not display a tear. The carriage rumbled away into the darkness.

Acknowledgments

There are many people in which I am thankful too in bringing the story of "Jack" to print. The first, and most important being God. For it is my belief that he planted the seed of Jack's story in my heart and mind over a decade ago. During that time I struggled with what it was he wanted me to write. Then he brought people into my life, some I sought out, others came to me. I believe a book is a collaboration of people with the author/creator.

The first was Sean Janson, a teacher and professor of English literature. Originally hired as a ghostwriter he taught me a lot of the craft of writing. He helped me over a span of four years, some with gaps due to world events and his health. God put the ability in me to write and Sean showed me where it was.

Next is Cyndy Brown who contributed with her poetry and prose. She captured the tone of the story and put it in pinpointed places throughout the entire story. This helped me see these characters and bring them alive.

Then there is Keith Francoeur. Keith illustrated the characters in the book which allowed me to picture them in my mind and bring them to life using words to describe not only their appearance but mannerisms as well.

Betsy Gold designed the origins of the cover and interior design to book one along with the logos for The Legend of Jack and Gotjack as well. She too had a good vision of the look and feel of the story and complimented it in her work.

Denise and Joel Aronson for editing and writing of the forward and draft manuscript of book one.

Jon at Best Price Signs and Designs for his help in designing the merchandise for both The Legend of Jack and Gotjack. He also helped in the fine tuning of both logos as well.

There are many others who along the way have encouraged me to keep at it when I wanted to quit. My family, friends, business people, and strangers who would come up to me in the grocery store, read one of the Jack phrases I was wearing that day and say, "Nice shirt!" I would like to thank everyone and ask them to keep it up for this is only book one and I have a desire to continue bringing the story of Jack to print.